———— ★ ————

CHAMBRUN'S FACE HAD THAT CARVED STONE LOOK TO IT

His eyes were like slits cut in a mask. "I damn well want to know what's going on up there on Fourteen."

Hardy's blond eyebrows rose. "You don't see any connection between this and the Watson kid, do you?"

"Marilyn saw something and got herself killed for that mishap," Chambrun said. "I suggest that Luther Downing saw something and got himself killed."

"You're playing games without any facts," Hardy said.

"I've learned one thing in a long life, Lieutenant. It may just be that there is no such thing in this world as a coincidence."

———— ★ ————

"Hugh Pentecost always provides the reader with top-notch storytelling."
—*Rave Reviews*

THE
FOURTEEN
DILEMMA
HUGH PENTECOST

TORONTO · NEW YORK · LONDON · PARIS
AMSTERDAM · STOCKHOLM · HAMBURG
ATHENS · MILAN · TOKYO · SYDNEY

THE FOURTEEN DILEMMA

A Worldwide Mystery/April 1990

First published by Dodd, Mead & Company, Inc.

ISBN 0-373-26045-8

Printed in U.S.A.

PART ONE

ONE

IN THE FAR WESTERN VILLAGE of Carlton's Creek the George Watson family were considered to be lucky beyond the average man's wildest dreams. They had won the state lottery. The big one this was. The proceeds included a quarter of a million dollars, to be paid at the rate of $25,000 a year for the next ten years; an expense-free week at New York's top luxury hotel, the Beaumont; free theaters and restaurants; new wardrobes for George and Helen Watson and their young daughter Marilyn; His and Her new compact cars when they got home. Security, luxury, the works; how lucky could you get?

Well, it turned out to be unlucky beyond that average man's conception. I know, because I was in the center of the horror that was visited on George and Helen Watson and their twelve-year-old daughter Marilyn.

I am the public relations man at the Hotel Beaumont in New York and have been for the last few years. I have seen violence at the Beaumont during that time. Why not? The Beaumont is like a small city within itself; shops, post office, banking facilities, its own hospital, restaurants, bars, theaters, convention halls, its own police force. The whole is presided over by that almost legendary manager, Pierre Chambrun. Chambrun is the manager, the mayor, the president,

the king—however you choose to look at him. More
about him later, because he, too, found himself in the
center of the Watsons' tragedy. There have been murders at the Beaumont in my time, as there are in any
small city. There have been robberies, fewer than in
most large hotels, thanks to a topflight security system. There are hookers to deal with, and deadbeats,
and con artists, and eager old gentlemen dying of
heart attacks in the wrong bedrooms with the wrong
ladies. There have been suicides. There has even been
a bombing. The Beaumont is a small city in motion.
According to Chambrun it is not just a hotel, but a
way of life. It is elegant, excruciatingly expensive, and
run with the interlocking perfection of a Swiss watch.

But, occasionally, things do go wrong. It is rarely
the hotel's own machinery that breaks down. What
goes wrong is imported from the outside, like a ve-
nereal disease brought home by a traveling salesman.
The hotel has to get rid of the infection, cleanse itself
of imperfections, and, above all, keep its public image intact. That last is my job.

There is one thing different about the Hotel Beaumont and a small city. Beyond a couple of dozen people who own cooperative apartments at the penthouse
level and the two top floors, it is a city inhabited by
people who are total strangers to each other, changing
day after day, week after week. They pay the tax, but
there are no town meetings. They may know a famous film star by name and sight, but they don't know
them and, by and large, they don't get to know them.
The only people who know each other well at the
Beaumont are Chambrun's people, his staff. Cham-

brun has a computer-type mind about his people. He knows all about all of them, from his fabulous executive secretary, Betsy Ruysdale, down to the third assistant dishwasher in the room service kitchen. He knows the names of their wives or husbands, their children, where they live, where they bank. If someone is in trouble, he knows it almost before the person knows it, and he will help if help is needed and deserved.

I mention this because the day the world caved in on George and Helen Watson, Chambrun wrote off his staff. The disaster had been imported from the outside and Chambrun never considered any other possibility.

I KEEP a sort of appointment-business diary in my office on the second floor, which adjoins my personal apartment, which adjoins Chambrun's suite of offices. I had a new book, a gift to me the Christmas of that year, with my name on the cover in gold letters— Mark Haskell. It was given to me by a lady I was in love with forever. I think you should know that I fall in love with someone forever about every six months. Each time I say goodbye to someone, with regret, it is because I think I have found the "right one," forever. The summer the Watsons came on their great free ride to New York, I had just said goodbye to the one who had given me the gold embossed business diary and found a new "right one forever." Her name was Carol Failes. I had cheered her with a rather corny pun, I remember. "I will not fail with Failes!" I was not failing with Failes at the moment, that was certain. Which is how Carol came to be involved with Helen Watson at the moment that disaster struck.

But I am getting ahead of myself.

In my business diary on the day of June 17th there is a list of seemingly unrelated items. (Let me say here that I don't keep any other kind of diary, a personal diary. No record of my triumphs or defeats. There was too much it was better to forget, and dreams of the future would have sounded childish. The most impossible of those dreams was that someday Chambrun would go into semi-retirement, become an elder statesman, and I would occupy the suite of offices down the hall. It was an absurd fantasy, because without Chambrun the Beaumont would cease to be the Beaumont and become nothing but another expensive rooming house.) My diary reminded me that on June 17th there would be a stamp auction in the mezzanine reception hall. I have never understood the fascination some people have for two-cent whatevers, but I was told that something close to a million dollars could change hands at that auction. In the Beaumont's beautiful little theater, also on the second floor, there was to be a preview of the first English-speaking film of France's leading sex-symbol, Yvonne Darcel. Yvonne, whose measurements you wouldn't believe, was occupying two suites on the fourteenth floor. With her were a husband, a young man reputed to be her current lover, her secretary and double. The double looked enough like Yvonne so that you had to take a good look to make certain which was which. I wouldn't have cared myself. There were also two sexy-looking maids who were supposed to keep Yvonne perpetually perfect in the public eye. There were some bawdy guesses being made backstage as to who was sleeping in what beds in those two suites—14A and 14B.

The diary also shows that there was to be a special luncheon in a private dining room for Nikos Parrasis, the multimillionaire Greek owner of half the world. He was in 14D, along with a bodyguard I suspected slept on the front door mat, guns in both hands and a knife in his teeth. The diary went on to remind me that the first round of the four-man International Bridge Championship was to be played in the small ball-room. The American team, four very intense young men, occupied 14F and 14G. Someone had dubbed them "the quadruplets." The black militant poet and playwright, Luther Downing, was to give a public reading of his latest odes to violence in the Jefferson Room to an audience of very rich and very poor intel-lectuals. Luther Downing was living it up in 14C; $240 a day, which is pretty heavy freight for your average poet. (That's without meals, booze, or stray women.)

Then, underlined in the diary, was the reminder that George and Helen Watson and their daughter Mari-lyn, winners of the lottery from Carlton's Creek in the foothills of the Rockies, would be arriving to occupy 14E. They were to get very careful red carpet treat-ment. The press, and the television cameras, and the radio microphones would be present in quantities. The Beaumont had to show that it knew how to play gra-cious host to this simple, all-American, super-lucky family.

Again, parenthetically, you have probably gotten
the hint that the fourteenth floor is a key locale in the
Watson saga. It is—was. There are ten suites on
Fourteen—A through J. They each consist of a living
room, serving pantry, two bedrooms and two baths.
These suites on Fourteen are never allocated to any
long-staying guests. They are for the super-rich, super-
celebrity, head-of-foreign-government type guest. A
week is about the time limit for occupying a Fourteen
suite. There was a constant turnover in VIPs. There
was sometimes a waiting list for Fourteen suites. For
example, the lady in 14J had waited three weeks to get
that precise suite. None of the others would do. When
George Atterbury, our reservation manager, asked her
why, she said it was because her name was Jasmine, J
for Jasmine. Her name was actually Mrs. Jasmine
Velasquez Gilhooly. On Chambrun's private file card
she was listed as "possibly the richest woman in the
world." That was reason enough to assign her to the
Fourteen suite of her choice. If she hadn't been about
seventy years old, I might have been more interested.
She could have bought the Beaumont without asking
the price.

There were two other Fourteen suites occupied.
Some sort of Arab sheik wearing his native headdress
was in 14H. His name was Abdel Ghorra. People
wearing the clothes and attitudes of another culture
were not rarities at the Beaumont. It was the home-
away-from-home of a lot of people with business at
the United Nations. Finally, in 14I there was a plain,
sandy-haired little man with wire-rimmed glasses who
was registered as Henry Bowers. He is what we call a

"John Smith" at the Beaumont. There was no reason
in the world for him to have been assigned a Fourteen
suite except that his reservation had been made by
somebody important in Washington. This meant that
"Bowers" was probably not his name, and that he was
from the FBI or the CIA or the IRS doing some kind
of gumshoe work for the Administration. I assumed
his assignment was the Arab sheik and didn't give
either of them a second thought until much later.

THE SUPER-LUCKY George Watsons arrived at the
Beaumont in the late afternoon of the 17th. A hotel
limousine had met them at the airport along with a
public relations man from their home state. I met them
at the registration desk. I was oozing charm, my job.

The Watsons were, somehow, not what I had
expected. I guess I thought they were going to be
farmers with cow manure on their boots. Instead they
looked like reasonably young, moderately sophisticated graduate students from their State university.
George was tall, and dark, and athletic-looking. His
sports jacket and slacks were off the rack somewhere
but chosen with a taste that avoided the gaudy. Helen
Watson was blonde, wearing a simple cotton frock
that, however, managed to show off a very good figure. Her face wasn't beautiful, but her smile was so
warm, her eyes so bright and friendly, her mouth so
generous, that she came off as rather special.

Marilyn Watson, the twelve-year-old daughter, was
a dream child. She reminded me of the Tenniel illus-
trations in an early *Alice in Wonderland* in my father's library. Her hair was blonde and hung down to

her waist. She looked around at the glitter and posh of the Beaumont lobby with her lips parted in wonder.

I introduced myself, told them I was their slave for their week's stay, urged them to name anything they wanted and I would provide it.

George Watson was just a little reserved, even hostile, I thought. He just said "Thanks," and signed up at the desk.

"I hope we're not going to be too much nuisance, Mr. Haskell," Helen Watson said. "This—this is all a little bit overwhelming. I'd like you to meet my daughter Marilyn."

Helen's hand was on the child's shoulder and she turned her my way. The child gave me an abbreviated curtsy and turned back to staring at the glass chandeliers overhead.

"Marilyn is retarded," Helen Watson said in a matter-of-fact voice; no apology, no regret, just a fact. "She doesn't hear and she can't speak."

"Maybe Mr. Haskell could provide you with a microphone so you could broadcast it to the whole damn world," George Watson said, angry. He had come up behind me.

Helen acted unrebuked, not hurt. "Mr. Haskell has to know why Marilyn doesn't respond when she's spoken to, George," she said. "So do the other hotel people who'll be involved with us." She smiled at me. "I hoped you might pass it along, Mr. Haskell, so I don't have to go into it every time a new person comes into the picture."

"Count on it," I said. My mouth felt a little dry. I was looking at Marilyn, who seemed poised on her patent leather toes, ready to fly up toward the chandeliers. What a ghastly thing for such a lovely child, so vitally alive.

The Watsons' luggage was brand-new, probably part of the lottery loot, I thought. I had a feeling there was more luggage than contents. I got that from Johnny Thacker, the day bell captain, who picked up a big suitcase and looked surprised by the heft of it.

Someone was tugging at my sleeve and I found myself confronted by the public relations man from the home state. His name was Henderson. He looked like a small-town drugstore cowboy, which I suspect was exactly what he was—used to whistling at the pretty girls.

"They're all yours," he said. "I picked up a chick on the plane east. I'm off to find her."

"'Into the valley of death—'" I quoted.

He grinned at me. "She seems pretty much alive," he said. "I don't know what's on the calendar, but maybe I should tip you off that George was an All-State athlete in his high school days; football, baseball. He might enjoy a game at Shea Stadium, the Mets or the Yanks or whoever's playing."

"The lady, too?" I asked.

His face clouded for a moment, as though my question mattered. "Her tastes are a little different," he said. "And, of course, she's hampered by the child."

An express elevator swept the Watsons, their luggage, two bellhops and me to Fourteen. We went down the hall to 14E. No two suites at the Beaumont are furnished alike. Fourteen E is early American. The two paintings on the wall, one a Benton, one a Wyeth, are not reproductions. Fourteen E is the epitome of elegant comfort. The furniture is solid and inviting, not like the gilt chairs in the Louis XIVth rooms down the hall.

George Watson seemed to take it all for granted, scowling around as if he was looking for something. A beer opener, I thought. I was working up a comfortable dislike for our friend George. Helen exclaimed with delight, recognized the paintings for what they were. The bellhops took the luggage down the corridor to the bedrooms and came back, hesitating. I signaled to them to take off.

"I should have tipped them, shouldn't I?" George said when they were gone.

"You are supposed to leave the Beaumont with your original dime in your pocket," I said.

That didn't seem to please him. "They'll think I'm some sort of a cheapskate," he said.

"Not when they pocket what the management has set aside for them," I said.

Marilyn was flitting around the room, touching everything. Not a sound came from her, but she kept turning to her mother, her eyes wide with excitement and pleasure.

The front doorbell rang and I went to answer it. Standing outside was Pierre Chambrun, accompanied by a room service waiter with a serving wagon. On the wagon was a bucket of ice with a champagne bottle imbedded. There was a tray of enticing canapés, and two small white boxes that I knew contained something from the hotel florist.

Chambrun is a short, square man with the brightest black eyes you ever saw peering out of deep pouches. Those eyes can be compassionate or turn your blood cold if he is angry. His manner and his appearance are as elegant as his hotel. He was wearing a dark blue, tropical worsted suit with a white carnation in his lapel. He walked into the suite, signaling the waiter to wheel in the wagon.

"Mr. and Mrs. Watson? I am Pierre Chambrun, the Beaumont's manager. I'm here to welcome you and to place myself at your service."

I was astonished. Kings and heads of states didn't normally rate this kind of recognition.

"Hi," George said, still looking for the beer opener, I thought.

"This is all so simply marvelous, Mr. Chambrun," Helen said.

He turned to the table and took up one of the small flower boxes. He opened it and took out a corsage of delicate young summer buds, perfect for a little girl. He advanced toward Marilyn with it. I tried to wigwag him, to warn him. I should have known better. He knew about Marilyn, just as he knew about everything that mattered in the Beaumont. He gave her a courtier's bow, gestured to her shoulder, asking permission to pin on the corsage, without speaking a word. Marilyn was delighted. She ran from her mother to her father, pointing to the flowers.

I thought Helen's eyes were suspiciously bright, tears near the surface. "How terribly sweet of you," she said to Chambrun.

He opened the second box. "Something a little more sophisticated for you, Mrs. Watson," he said. It was a yellow orchid, surrounded by lilies-of-the valley. "The champagne is for later, when you are rested and refreshed. Anything the Beaumont can supply is yours for the asking. Just tell Mark what it is." He gave me his professional smile. "If he doesn't hop to it, I promise you I will feed him to the lions."

So the visit of the lucky Watsons began.

We had tickets for them to the Broadway musical *Shenandoah* for that night. They dined in their own suite. At the moment it was time for them to take off for the theater in a hotel limousine Helen Watson reneged.

"Marilyn won't be able to hear anything," she told me. "I don't think—"

"I never heard anyone say they were going to 'hear' a play," I said. "They always say they are going to 'see' a play. There will be so much for her to see: the lights, the costumes, the dancing, the audience."

I persuaded her. I would have liked to go with them to watch the child's reactions, but I had other chores. When they came back, Helen and the child were beaming. George looked glum. I suspected there weren't the kind of naked chorus girls in *Shenandoah* he'd hoped for.

The plan was for them to take in the after-theater show in the Beaumont's Blue Lagoon Room. Again Helen backed off. Marilyn had had enough excitement for one night. I said we had already arranged for a baby sitter. Helen compromised. She would go up

with Marilyn, and if the child seemed comfortable
with the sitter, she'd join us in the Blue Lagoon. Put
that way, I decided that left me holding George's hand
until Helen made up her mind. Then I had a brain
wave of my own. Carol Failes, the girl I was in love
with forever, had sublet an apartment just a block
from the hotel. She had sublet it from a girl I had once
been in love with forever. I gave Carol a call and invited her to make a fourth for the balance of the evening.

Mr. Cardoza, the maître d' in the Blue Lagoon, had
given us a number one table, front and center. George
Watson didn't seem very much interested in Johnny
Felton's soft and subtle rendition of show tunes from
the golden age of Cole Porter, Gershwin, Kern, and
Berlin on the grand piano. This was between shows. I
figured George hadn't been born when those tunes
were popular and I told myself he probably wasn't interested in anything that had happened before he'd
made his entrance, front and center, at Carlton's
Creek. He ordered a rye and ginger ale. I saw the
waiter wince. I don't imagine anybody had ordered
that combination in the Blue Lagoon since the days of
prohibition.

There was a stir a few tables away and a lot of people began talking at once. Then there was some ap-
plause, not directed at the stage. Yvonne Darcel had
made an entrance, accompanied by her husband and
her boy friend. She was wearing a full black skirt and
a lace top you could see through from the navel up.

George Watson whistled. I should have known he
would.

"Who's the chick?" he asked.

"French movie star," I said.

"I never go to foreign films. Makes me restless not to understand the language," George said.

He probably couldn't read the subtitles, I told myself. I was working up a real hate on George Watson.

And it got worse. We'd just started on our first round of drinks when Mr. Cardoza brought Carol Failes over to our table. Carol is a really lovely girl; red hair God had given her, a figure that might have made Mlle. Darcel a little envious, and gray-green eyes that reminded me of the Irish Sea on a summer day. I introduced her to George and he took both her hands in his and his face lit up.

"Now we're getting somewhere," he said.

The sonofabitch was moving right in on me. He wasn't much of a conversationalist, but he talked. It wasn't long before he got around to the four touchdowns he scored against Gillespie High for the State Championship twelve years ago. I had to think nothing much else had happened to him since then. Of course there had been Helen and Marilyn. Carol, looking at me with dancing eyes, got him around to the lottery, and how it must be changing his life, and what was he going to do with all that bread. It turned out he thought of opening a sporting goods store in Carlton's Creek.

Carol gave my hand a reassuring squeeze under the table. George wondered if there wasn't someplace we could go to dance. He was imagining himself giving Carol a workout.

Then, thank God, Helen joined us. Marilyn had been quite content with the baby sitter.

"I wanted you to meet Carol," I told her, "because you and she are going to spend a good part of tomorrow together."

"Oh?"

"I am supposed to help you select your new wardrobe, Mrs. Watson," Carol told Helen. "In the morning a lot of things will be brought to your suite to select from. I'll have a girl come to model some dresses for you, if you want. Then, if you haven't found what you really like, we'll spend the afternoon taking a look at some of the best places in town."

"You got some chick who will help me pick out my clothes, Haskell?" George asked.

"We'll turn you loose in Barney's Boys Town," I said. "In the afternoon you can occupy the hotel's box at Shea Stadium—Yankees and the Red Sox."

"But no chick?" He laughed. Big joke.

Carol's aim in life is to become a high fashion dress designer, maybe have her own line of clothes. She was getting some practical experience with marketing in the hotel's boutique. I had maneuvered her into handling Mrs. Watson's new wardrobe, mostly because it meant I would see more of her. She and Helen seemed to hit it off very well. They chattered away about clothes, and fashions, and new styles. George retired into his personal gloom. It was just about time for the midnight show when George came out of it with a bang.

He stood up so abruptly that he jarred the table and knocked over his wife's drink.

"That bastard!" he said.

He was staring across the room at a couple sitting at a corner table. They were from out of town. You could tell that from a mile away. The man was owlish-looking in horn-rimmed glasses. The woman was a familiar sub-suburban housewife type. The man had spotted George and he bent down to say something to the woman. She looked up quickly at George, and then away quickly.

Helen had reached out to take hold of George's arm. "Please, George!" she said urgently.

He shook her off and started across the room.

Helen looked at me, frightened. "Someone from back home that George doesn't like very much," she said. "I hope there won't be trouble."

Mr. Cardoza, the maître d', sees all, knows all. I gave him a high sign and before George reached the table where the man he didn't like was rising to his feet, three waiters were very busy doing nothing in that area.

We couldn't hear what anyone was saying, of course, but it was obvious that George was doing most of the talking. The woman had risen, too, and was clinging to her escort's arm. Then George turned on his heel and walked out of the Blue Lagoon, never once looking at his wife, or Carol, or me. He was a dark storm headed for somewhere else. The couple across the room were paying their check. Whatever had been about to happen wasn't going to happen, I thought.

What none of us knew was that the clock was ticking steadily down toward the zero hour for disaster.

TWO

How or where I spent the rest of that night has nothing much to do with this story. It is part of my routine to be in Chambrun's office at precisely nine o'clock in the morning. When I arrive, he is always just finishing his breakfast, which, for him is a major meal. It consists of fresh juice, steak or lamb chops, sometimes scrambled eggs added, sometimes a creamed finnan haddie in place of the meat, hash browned potatoes, one slice of a hot-house tomato, gluten toast with sweet butter, and a spoonful of strawberry jam made by some friends in Devonshire, England. He drinks two cups of American coffee and then goes to a foul Turkish brew which Miss Ruysdale prepares in a special coffee maker on the sideboard. In my judgment you're lucky if you aren't asked to share that delicacy with him. Chambrun doesn't eat again until dinnertime, and that is always a gourmet delight prepared by Jacques Fresney, the hotel's master chef, served either in the office or in Chambrun's penthouse on the roof.

At precisely nine o'clock Chambrun pushes back his chair from the breakfast table, crosses to his desk, and lights his second Egyptian cigarette of the day. Waiting for him are a stack of registration cards brought up to date by Miss Ruysdale. These are the people who have registered since yesterday morning. The Beau-

mont's guests might have been a little disturbed had
they known how total the information was we had on
them. Little symbols, placed on the cards by Miss
Ruysdale, give us their credit ratings, whether the
guest is an alcoholic, a woman or man chaser, a husband double-crossing his wife, or a wife two-timing
her husband, home town information of any use to us,
political information if the guest is in politics or government, police records, if any. My job is to know
what guests want publicity and those who don't. A
movie star from the West Coast may want a flag run
up or may want complete privacy. The same goes for
bank presidents and foreign diplomats. Local gossip
columnists are on my back every day to find out who
is new in the world of the Beaumont, and it's my re-
sponsibility to leak only the information that our
guests want me to leak.

That morning of June 18th was a beautiful, warm,
sunny summer day, the kind of day that made you
want to play hooky. There was nothing of any particular interest or significance in the collection of registration cards Chambrun and I looked over. He put
them to one side and asked me about the Watsons.

"Today is wardrobe day," I said. "Carol Failes is
taking care of the lady. Watson is on his own, with a
blank check, so to speak, at Brooks Brothers."

Chambrun gave me a small smile. "That worked
out rather nicely for you," he said.

"I don't follow."

"Involving Miss Failes," he said.

"She's just right for the job," I said.

"I'm sure. What about the press?"

"I'm trying to keep them from following us around," I said. "I don't want the other guests disturbed by them. I've set up a special session for photographers tomorrow morning, interviews and all that."

"I gather there was some minor trouble last night," he said.

I have the feeling that Chambrun has a special built-in radar system. He knows everything that goes on in the Beaumont, even though it doesn't seem important. Mr. Cardoza, the maître d' in the Blue Lagoon, must have reported George Watson's small run-in with "the couple from home."

"Nothing really happened," I said. "I didn't see Watson again afterwards. He took off somewhere."

"He came back into the hotel shortly before three A.M.," Chambrun said. "Very drunk, but able to make it to Fourteen without a scene."

"He's a jerk," I said.

"He's a guest of the hotel," Chambrun reminded me.

Guests of the hotel could do the most outrageous things, provided they didn't disturb other guests, and ask for the most outrageous services from the staff, provided again that those services didn't interfere with the perfect functioning of the hotel's machinery.

I was reminded of that when I got to my office, down the hall from Chambrun's. My secretary had left a memo on my desk.

Mrs. Jasmine Velasquez Gilhooly asks that you
join her in her suite, 14J, at 11:30 this morning to
discuss matters of importance.

My secretary, a gal named Vanessa, who just possibly might be someone I could fall in love with forever some months from now—after Carol, God forbid
that there should be an after—had come in to look
over my shoulder.

"I told her it was unlikely you could make it at
eleven-thirty," Vanessa said. "I told her you had the
lucky Watsons to cope with. She suggested you cope
with them at some other time than eleven-thirty. I said
I would pass on the suggestion."

"Demanding old bitch!" I said.

There were other routines that morning—arrang-
ing certain press interviews; a fashion show setup; re-
checking on the International Bridge Tournament; a
dozen other parts of the day's program.

I did call Jasmine Velasquez Gilhooly about ten-
thirty. I had never had a conversation with the lady,
although I'd seen her, weighted down with rings and
necklaces, hennaed hair, summer furs. Her voice, the
product of too many cigarettes and too much liquor,
was a surprise. It didn't seem to come from the dow-
ager duchess I expected. It seemed to ride over humor.

"If you are the blond Adonis I've seen around the
hotel with Pierre, I'll have to curb my impatience,"
she said. "Will you call me when you can make it?"

"Blond Adonis" is not a bad way to approach a
man of thirty-five. Calling Chambrun by his first

name was another rather potent gambit. I promised to call her.

"Perhaps a cocktail before lunch?" she suggested. "My health requires a vodka martini on the rocks about a quarter to one."

"I'll do my level best," I said.

She chuckled. "And don't bring that lovely red-head with you, Mark. At my age I can't take that kind of competition."

Maybe she just called everybody by their first names, but I thought I better check out. I dialed Miss Ruysdale's extension.

Someday somebody is going to write a feature about Betsy Ruysdale for a woman's magazine. She's handsome in the true meaning of the word, ageless as every woman between thirty and fifty is supposed to be. She dresses expensively but not seductively. Chambrun wouldn't want every male in the establishment salivating over his secretary. As his secretary she is unbelievable. She reads his mind, she anticipates his every need. I have never known her not to be precisely where she was needed when she was needed. Chambrun calls her, simply, Ruysdale—never Betsy or Miss Ruysdale. It sort of neuters her, and yet—and yet—there are people who whisper that she just may supply Chambrun with a good deal more than business efficiency. If she does, it is handled with incredible discretion and total secrecy.

"I have a command performance from the lady in Fourteen," I told Miss Ruysdale.

"Mrs. Jasmine Gilhooly?" Miss Ruysdale chuckled.

"She calls the boss by his first name," I said.

"Not presumptuous," Betsy said. "I understand it was a near thing about thirty years ago." She sounded suddenly demure. "That was well before my time, of course."

"Thirty years ago you were playing with dolls," I said.

"Thank you, sir. The lady was the widow of Sebastian Velasquez, the Spanish tycoon. The boss was a dashing young hero out of the French Resistance. She could have bought the hotel for him if he'd said 'yes.' It happens he said 'no.'"

"So they are friends," I said. "Was she attractive in those days?"

"She used to get paid for taking off her clothes," Betsy said.

"Come again!"

"She was a stripper," Betsy said. "Old burlesque days. From what I hear she made Gypsy Rose Lee look like an amateur."

"Now I've heard everything!"

"When the boss said 'no' our Jasmine turned to Francis Xavier Gilhooly, a contractor specializing in condominiums. He died in bed with Jasmine, but, as the man said, 'what a way to go.' He left her owning half the retirement homes around the world. She is just plain, lousy rich, Mark. I suggest you keep your date with her. It would please the boss if you can do something she wants, and you just might find her quite refreshing."

I decided that a vodka martini on the rocks with the unexpected Jasmine might be fun, but I never made it—that is, not at a quarter to one. By then I was in the clutches of a sickening anxiety.

It started at a little after eleven. I was still in my office when I got a call from Carol.

"I have missed you unbearably since the last time I saw you," I told her. The last time I'd seen her had been at breakfast in her apartment.

She didn't respond quite the way I'd expected. She sounded tense. "We have a little trouble up here, Mark."

"Mrs. Watson doesn't like the clothes you picked out for her?"

"It's Marilyn," Carol said. "She—she's wandered off somewhere."

"Wandered off?"

"Helen Watson and I were trying on clothes in the bedroom. There's a full-length mirror there. Marilyn watched for a while, and then went off into the living room. There wasn't any reason to check on her, so we don't know exactly when she took off. It could have been as much as a half-hour ago. Not more. I thought maybe you could alert the hotel security people—"

"Sure," I said. "Call you back when we find her. She can't have got very far."

I didn't feel even a touch of concern, which shows you the kind of crystal ball I work with. The Beaumont was full of amazing wonders for a twelve-year-old who'd never been out of Carlton's Creek before. I remembered her open-mouthed wonder when they'd arrived yesterday, staring up at the glittering cut-glass chandeliers in the lobby. There were the shops, and the people, and the express elevators and God knows what else to fascinate her. I called Jerry Dodd, our security chief. Jerry is a dark, wiry little man who can lick twice his weight in wildcats if he has to. He runs a very tight ship at the Beaumont. I like to think that Ruysdale, Jerry and I are the three people on the staff Chambrun counts on without reservations.

"I wouldn't make a federal case of it," I told Jerry when I'd reported on Marilyn, "except that the child has problems. She can't hear and she can't speak. She couldn't ask anyone how to get back to Fourteen if she got lost."

"What does she look like?" Jerry asked.

"Alice in Wonderland," I said.

"Never met her," Jerry said. "Come on, Mark!"

"Blonde hair, hanging down to her waist. Slender, rather tall for her age, which is twelve. I don't know what she's wearing, but it would be a simple little girl's dress."

"We should find her in a few minutes," Jerry said.

"Call Mrs. Watson in Fourteen E if you can't locate me," I said. "I'll be looking around."

I walked down to the lobby, which was busy. The lunch hour was approaching. I sometimes think half the city's business is conducted over cocktails and lunch in the Beaumont's various dining areas. I spotted Johnny Thacker, the day bell captain. He remembered Marilyn from yesterday's check-in, but he hadn't seen her this morning.

"Of course I've been off the floor several times with new arrivals," Johnny said. "I'll ask around."

I did some asking around myself. Nobody on the front desk had seen her, no one in the shops or anyplace else on the lobby level. I still wasn't too concerned. She probably hadn't come downstairs at all. She could still be wandering around somewhere on Fourteen. I checked each elevator operator and none of them remembered seeing Marilyn, so she still had to be upstairs somewhere.

I went up to Fourteen. The housekeeper, Mrs. Kniffin, and the maids on that floor had already been looking for the child at Helen Watson's request. They'd found no sign of her.

Well, there were other ways beside the elevators for her to have left Fourteen, most obvious being the fire stairs. She could have gone up or down.

I checked in at 14E. One look at Helen Watson's drawn face told me they had no news. Carol looked pretty badly shaken herself. I think that was when I first felt a little knot forming in the pit of my stomach.

"Does she often wander off like this?" I asked Helen.

"There's never been anything like this," she said. "I mean, this is the first time in a strange place, away from home. At home she'd go off into the woods, or walk down into the village. Everybody back home knows her. There were never any restrictions on her going where she felt like going." Her voice broke. "There's little enough else for her."

"So she wouldn't feel guilty about wandering off," I said. "So she'll wander back when it suits her. She may be handicapped, Helen, but she strikes me as being more than average bright."

"She sees everything, notices everything," Helen said. "She wouldn't be easily lost."

Carol had moved over by the windows. "I've been wondering, Mark. She could see the Park from here—people riding on the bridle paths. She seemed quite excited about it. Do you suppose—?"

I started to say Marilyn would have had to go through the lobby to get to the Park, but the sudden look of hope on Helen Watson's face cut that off.

"We can have a look over there," I said. "You'd better stay here, Helen, in case someone brings her back. Don't worry too much. This is a pretty big haystack."

Carol and I went out into the hall together, ostensibly to have a look in the Park. In addition to the horseback riders there were kids playing games, flying kites. Marilyn could logically have been attracted to them. I didn't see how she could have gone through the lobby and out one of the two main doors, watched over by doormen, without being noticed, but it was possible, I supposed.

Carol and I were walking toward the elevators and I could feel her fingers biting into my arm. She was hanging onto me for dear life.

"I'm not going with you, Mark, but I wanted to talk to you away from Helen. She may be going to need someone with her."

I stopped walking and looked down at this girl I was in love with forever—for now, at least. She's a nice girl, Carol. She has a genuine compassion for people.

"It's crazy, but I keep wondering, Mark," she said.

"So wonder to me," I said. I touched her cheek with my fingers. She felt cool, nice. She smelled nice.

"There's been so much publicity about the Watsons," she said. "All that money, Mark. Do you suppose someone just waited their chance and took Marilyn?"

"A kidnapping?" That was a dimension that hadn't occurred to me.

"That means Helen would be hearing: a phone call, a note."

I tried to make it fit. No one could have dragged Marilyn out through the lobby and onto the street. That would have been more noticeable than the child alone. But a kidnapper could have taken the child down the fire stairs, or in a service elevator, and out one of the basement exits. It was even possible that could have been done without their being seen, if the kidnapper knew the geography of the hotel, the sub-basement floor plan. A quick buck by violence was part of our world these days.

But it was pretty far-out. "I'll take a look in the Park, or have someone else take a look," I said. "There's really no reason why anyone should have stopped the child if she was wandering around. She isn't a baby. If they didn't know about her problems—"

I left Carol there on Fourteen and went down to the lobby. No news there. I ran into Jerry Dodd. None of his people had turned anything up. He didn't seem terribly concerned until I suggested Carol's theory to him. His black eyes stared intently at me for a moment or two while he weighed it.

"I checked out with the kitchen staff on the phone," he said. "Nobody down there has seen her. How much money did these people win, Mark?"

"A quarter of a million in cash plus a lot of fringe benefits—like the free ride here."

"That's a lot of bread," he said. "Let me ask some different questions of people. I'll be in touch."

But he wasn't in touch for quite a while. I checked in with Ruysdale. Nothing cooking there. So I went for a walk in the Park. It was a delightful day, hot but not humid. Flowers were in bloom. Kids played happily. It was an ideal day to be out, an ideal place to be. I asked around but nobody had seen a lonely Alice in Wonderland.

It doesn't take long to tell, but by the time I went back to the hotel and up to Chambrun's office, Marilyn Watson had been missing for a couple of hours.

Chambrun was brisk and businesslike about it. He reminded me of an axiom of his about the hotel business. "The impossible is always quite possible."

There had been just the right moment for Marilyn to slip out of the hotel unnoticed. If she had tried to be "unnoticed," a dozen people would have seen her. Since she wasn't trying, there had been just the right combination of circumstances, people coming and going, a doorman a few yards from his post whistling for a taxi. She had slipped out into the city.

"She had seen plenty of flowers and kids playing in Carlton's Creek," Chambrun said, "but never a Madison Avenue bus or a pawnshop or a big department store."

"We'd better call the local police precinct house," I said.

"Done forty minutes ago," Chambrun said. "They'll bring her back." He turned to his Turkish coffee and a stack of papers on his desk.

There were things I'd neglected, most noticeably a luncheon for the local Republican Women's Club. I went to make sure everything was in order there, that the arrangements I'd made for press and photographers were working properly. I glanced at my watch and realized I'd missed my appointment with Jasmine Velasquez Gilhooly. I had Mr. Quiller, the maître d' in charge of the luncheon, call her to tell her I'd been caught in an emergency and apologize for me. The lady running the lunch—I believe in this day and age she is called the chairperson—wanted the microphones for the speakers to be placed differently. This meant locating the chief electrician and giving him instructions. It took time. I waited around for the after-lunch speeches to begin, saw that everything was functioning, and took off. I was just leaving the private dining room when I saw Johnny Thacker, the bell captain, flagging me.

"You're wanted in the boss's office," he told me. He looked strangely pale. "They've found the kid."

"Thank God," I said, relieved.

"Don't thank Him yet," Johnny said. A nerve twitched at the corner of his mouth. "She's dead."

I just stared at him, the knot yanking tight in my stomach.

"Somebody smashed in her skull and jammed her body into the trash barrel outside the service elevator on Fourteen. Not fifty feet from the door to the Watsons' suite."

"Oh, Jesus!" I remember saying.

THREE

THERE ARE NOT many believable reasons why anyone would murder a twelve-year-old child who can't hear or speak. Her parents might want to get rid of her, which is a pretty grotesque notion. My girl Carol had been with Helen Watson, had seen Marilyn alive, and hadn't left Helen's side until two hours after the child had disappeared when she'd walked out to the elevators with me. Watson had been shopping at Brooks Brothers and was at a ball game in Shea Stadium. So that notion didn't hold up.

It was possible some sex freak had found Marilyn wandering around, dragged her into the service area, raped her, killed her, and jammed her body into the trash barrel. That one stayed high on the list for a while.

There was a third possible answer that also rated high. Marilyn had seen something that was dangerous to someone, for example a hotel thief at work. I'm getting ahead of myself a little when I tell you that no one on the fourteenth floor reported anything missing, or any signs that anyone had been interrupted in the process of trying to steal anything.

Yet it was almost certain that Marilyn had been killed on the fourteenth floor, only a few yards from the suite where her mother and Carol were selecting a wardrobe, part of the lottery loot. It wasn't sensible to assume that she'd been killed somewhere else in the hotel and brought back to the trash barrel on Fourteen. So all the tenants and the staff on Fourteen became the primary suspects in this senseless horror.

I think I have broken off telling the story in sequence at this point because I don't like to remember the next piece of time after Johnny Thacker broke the news to me. I know I ran up the stairway and down the hall to Chambrun's office. Ruysdale wasn't at her desk. I barged into Chambrun's office and found him sitting at his desk, looking like a hanging judge. I had the cockeyed notion that something had gone wrong with the air conditioning. The room felt cold. I was surprised to find Chambrun alone. I had expected a whirlwind of activity.

"You've heard?" he said in a flat voice. His eyes glittered in their deep pouches.

I nodded. "Do you know who—?"

"We don't know a goddamned thing yet," Chambrun said. "Ruysdale has gone up to break the news to Mrs. Watson. Quite frankly I chickened out on it till there's something more to tell her than the stark fact."

I heard someone come into the office behind me and I turned to face a girl from the stenographic pool. I knew her by sight but not by name. Chambrun knows everyone's name.

"You're to handle the telephones at Miss Ruysdale's desk, Miss Simmons," he said. "You know what's happened?"

She was chalk white. "Mr. Dodd told me, sir."

"No one is to come in here without your checking with me except Ruysdale, Dodd, and Lieutenant

Hardy of the police. I'm not here to any phone calls unless they're connected with this business."

"Yes, sir." Miss Simmons went out to man the barricade.

"Hardy's here?" I asked.

"We got lucky," Chambrun said.

Lieutenant Hardy of Manhattan's Homicide Division is an old friend. He is a big blond man who looks more like a confused professional football linebacker than a very shrewd detective. He is a slow but very dogged investigator who never lets a grain of sand slip through his fingers without examining it. He and Chambrun have a mutual respect for each other; the one thorough, step by step, never letting go; the other intuitive, often ignoring details, not concerned with legal technicalities, arriving at answers by short cuts the other wouldn't dream of taking. They have complemented each other in the past. Murder isn't unheard-of at the Beaumont. I've said, it's like a small city.

"Who found her?" I asked.

"There's a regular trash collection about one-thirty," Chambrun said. "One of the custodial staff, a man named Metzger, stopped the service elevator at Fourteen to empty the trash barrel. She was there."

"Skull bashed in, Johnny Thacker told me."

"Like a pumpkin run over by a truck."

"Why, for God sake?"

Chambrun looked at me with such a cold fury that I wondered, for an insane moment, if he thought I had done it.

"A child who couldn't even call for help!" he said. He was holding a pencil between his squarish fingers and it suddenly snapped in two. He looked down at it, surprised. Then he picked up the pieces and dropped them in his wastebasket. Heavy lids hooded his eyes. "So much for emotions," he said in a dangerously quiet voice. "Your Miss Failes is a starting point, Mark. She may be the last person beside Marilyn's mother and the murderer to see the child alive. Try to get her to avoid hysterics."

"She's not the hysterical type."

"She made the identification for Jerry Dodd. You haven't seen the body—and I advise against developing any curiosity on the subject. It's an altogether ghastly sight. Your young lady is going to give way at some point. It would be helpful if she could answer questions first." The red light on his desk phone blinked. He picked it up and said after a moment, "Send him in, Miss Simmons."

The door opened and Dr. Partridge, our house physician, came in. He is a tall, gaunt, gray old man who always sounds impatient. He spends most of his time playing backgammon with some cronies in the Spartan Bar, and whenever he is called on professionally, he reacts with outrage. I thought he looked more than usually shaken that afternoon. He ignored me.

"I have a dream that I'll get a crack at the bastard who did this before they lock him up," Doc Partridge said.

"You'll have to stand in line," Chambrun said.

"The Medical Examiner's got the body," Doc said. "Hardy's people are looking for the weapon. No sign of anything yet. The shocking violence of it, Pierre! It had to be something heavy, an iron pipe, God knows what.''

"Was she sexually attacked?" Chambrun asked.

"You'll have to wait for something definitive from the M.E. My examination was superficial. My guess is that she wasn't. That whole goddamn floor is a madhouse. Everyone has an urgent appointment somewhere and they're all screaming at Hardy to let them go. The only one who's keeping her cool is that crazy old broad who once had her eye on you, Pierre, a few years back.''

"Jasmine? That was thirty years back, Doc."

"Seems like yesterday," Doc said. "When you get to be my age, everything seems like yesterday. There's some Arab creep running around in his burnoose claiming diplomatic immunity, four guys who have to get to a bridge game, and that French tootsie with her boys and gals screaming that they have to go to the preview of her latest film. Then there's that Greek Midas with his bodyguard who threatened to shoot a cop when he demanded in. And there's the black poet who's telling everyone he will be blamed for it because he's black! It's wild.''

"A man named Henry Bowers?" Chambrun asked.

Doc shrugged. "He and George Watson are the only ones missing at the moment."

"Did you have a look at Mrs. Watson?"

"Poor damned woman is like carved out of ice," Doc said. "It's like she didn't believe it had happened. Mark's girl friend is helping to hold her together. I guess you could say they're helping each other to stay in one piece."

"You give her a sedative?"

Doc shook his head. "She won't hear of it. There might be something she can do, though God knows what she means by that."

It was, as Chambrun said somewhere along the way, like weaving a tapestry: a thread here, another there, a crisscrossing of a third. Only the threads were people, jumbled together in a place that was unfamiliar to them—one floor in the Beaumont. Some of them were just window dressing, some, like the Watsons, were deeply involved in the basic scene, and one of them, the blood washed off his hands so that they looked innocent, was at the core of an unimaginable violence.

One of the things I had learned long ago, when I'd first started to work for Chambrun, was that the difference between the faces people wore in the world of the Beaumont and what lay behind them is in sharper contrast than you find in everyday life. Because the Beaumont sure as hell isn't everyday. There is no one in the world of the Beaumont wearing a frayed collar and wondering if he can pay the grocer; there are no underprivileged; there are none of the expected turmoils you find in a slum. The stage setting of the hotel is cool, elegant, efficiently put together and operated. Furs and jewels and clothes beyond the pocketbook of the average man are commonplace. A guest raises a finger and says, "Bring me—" and it is brought, because it is taken for granted his wallet is stuffed with money to pay for the champagne, or

black caviar, or an air-conditioned limousine to take
him five blocks, or cold fresh salmon flown in from
the Northwest. The most expensive call girls in the
world sip frosted drinks in the Trapeze Bar, ready to
satisfy more exotic tastes. Behind all this you sense
power, and intrigue, and romance. But you come to
know that all that glitter conceals the same petty
meannesses, the same greeds and jealousies and lusts,
the same treacheries, the same impulses to cruelty, the
same potential for dark violence, that inhabit the less
fortunate, the poor, the hungry, the exploited, the
traditional villains, the traditional psychotics. Dia-
mond rings don't keep a woman from drugs or alco-
holism; a valet to lay out his clothes doesn't keep a
man from cheating and stealing and indulging in sexual perversions. The elegant façade shouldn't make
the discovery of what lies behind it astonishing. People are people.

So now we had to pry beneath the lacquered sur-
faces to find a man, or woman, who had brutally
eliminated an innocent child. Along the way we would
almost certainly uncover the hidden cesspools in a
dozen hearts.

The first chipping away at that surface was begun by
Lieutenant Hardy, who came into the office while Doc
Partridge was still there, accompanied by Mrs. Grace
Kniffin, the housekeeper on Fourteen. Hardy, typi-
cally, began at the beginning. How could it have happened, in broad daylight, at eleven o'clock in the
morning, with Mrs. Kniffin and her staff of maids
busy on the floor, people coming and going?

Mrs. Kniffin was an old-timer at the hotel, a nice, gray-haired, motherly woman. Chambrun was God to her, and his reassuring nod told her he didn't hold her responsible. That was all she needed to shed her anxieties.

"It was an ordinary morning," Mrs. Kniffin said. And then her eyes widened as she realized the absurdity of her comment. An "ordinary morning" in which a child had been bludgeoned to death within a few yards of where she, Mrs. Kniffin, must have been.

The patient Hardy nodded. "I drew a little diagram of the floor," he said. "There are five suites down each side of the corridor. A to E on the east side, F to J on the west side. On the north end of the corridor are windows looking out over the city. No fire escape there—straight drop of fourteen floors to the street. We can forget the windows. At the south end we have a bank of elevators—four; the door to the service area, the elevator there, and the fire stairs. That's how you'd have to come and go; the four passenger elevators, the service elevator, the fire stairs. Then there is the linen room which, in effect, is your office, your domain, Mrs. Kniffin."

"Yes, sir."

"When the door to the linen room is open, you can see straight down the corridor to the windows at the north end. You can see the doors to each one of the ten suites."

"Yes, sir."

"So let's go to just before eleven o'clock, Mrs. Kniffin, and take the next half-hour of time. Where were you? What did you see? Who did you see? And before we begin, did you see any strangers, visitors to the suites, anyone you didn't recognize as belonging on Fourteen?"

"No one," Mrs. Kniffin said.

Chambrun leaned forward. "You're positive, Mrs. Kniffin?"

"Positive, sir. But—" She let it hang there.

"But what, Mrs. Kniffin?" Hardy asked.

"It doesn't mean there wasn't anyone," Mrs. Kniffin said. "Fourteen is a difficult floor, as you well know, Mr. Chambrun."

Chambrun nodded. He knew every detail of every operation in the Beaumont. "From a housekeeper's point of view," he said to Hardy. "Those are superluxury suites on Fourteen. The people who occupy them aren't apt to be up and out early in the morning. That means that the housekeeper and the maids often have to wait till lunchtime to get into the rooms to clean, make the beds, put out fresh linen and towels. Mrs. Kniffin and her maids have to wait till someone goes out, then they pounce on that particular suite and do their job. I think you should know, Lieutenant, that Mrs. Kniffin doesn't stand guard in the linen room watching the corridor. When the maids are free to go into a suite, Mrs. Kniffin will eventually follow them in, double-check on the condition of things. The fact that she didn't see anyone she couldn't account for doesn't mean there was no one. While she was in one of the suites—" He shrugged.

"Were there any special problems this morning?" Hardy asked.

Mrs. Kniffin gave the detective a tired little smile. "There are always problems," she said. "This morning?" She ticked the problems off on her fingers. "We first got into F and G, the two suites occupied by the gentlemen bridge players. There were cigarette burns in a sheet there. The maids sent for me. Then one of the maids came yelling for me. She had knocked on the door of the Greek gentleman's suite, that's D. When no one answered, she used her pass key to go in and found herself facing the bodyguard, who was pointing a gun at her! I had to calm her down and apologize to Mr. Parrasis. Then there was Mrs. Gilhooly in J. That faces A on the west side of the corridor. She was complaining about the French movie star and her crowd in A and B. Loud quarreling and shouting at each other."

"I thought the rooms were soundproofed," Hardy said.

"They are—if the doors are closed," Mrs. Kniffin said. "That French actress and her crowd come and go from A to B. They don't use the connecting door on the inside. So they come and go by the corridor doors. They probably aren't quarreling; just talking French."

Chambrun smiled, a small, crooked smile. "Mrs. Gilhooly speaks French fluently," he said. "She would know whether they were quarreling or not."

"I suppose that could be," Mrs. Kniffin said. "Finally there was a complaint from the French actress herself. No clean towels in one of the bathrooms in B. She's supposed to be in A, but she was in B, screaming at me. There had been clean towels the night before; I'd checked it myself. But there were no clean towels this morning. In fact there were no towels at all. They'd all been carried into the second bathroom by someone. Of course she blamed us and of course we apologized and got more towels for her.''

"And while you were covering all those bases you didn't see anyone strange, suspicious, anyone who shouldn't have been there?'' Hardy asked.

"No one,'' Mrs. Kniffin said.

"And you didn't see Marilyn Watson wandering around?''

A look of horror came over Mrs. Kniffin's face. "I never saw her, sir.''

Hardy was studying the little notebook in which he'd drawn his diagram of the floor. "The child came out of Suite E, which is at the far end of the corridor on the east side,'' he said. "She had to cover the full length of the corridor to the service area. Someone either picked her up in the hall or in the service area itself. Neither you nor your maids saw her?''

"No, sir.''

"There are two maids, right? When were you all together, out of the hall?''

"In the room where the cigarette burns were,'' Mrs. Kniffin said. "That was in F. Later we were all in the French lady's suite—B.''

"But didn't somebody go to get fresh towels?''

"Yes. Amy went to the linen room.''

"And she didn't see Marilyn?''

"Positively not, Lieutenant.''

I knew what Hardy was thinking. Somewhere in that short stretch of time between eleven and eleven-thirty, with maids and people coming and going,

Marilyn Watson had come out of Suite E unseen, gone down the hall unseen, been grabbed by someone, bludgeoned, murdered, jammed into the trash barrel—all unseen, and yet with maids and guests only a few yards away. Some evil guardian angel had been on the side of the killer.

Miss Simmons opened the office door. "There is a Mr. Downing to see you and the lieutenant, Mr. Chambrun," she said.

Standing behind her was Luther Downing, the militant black poet. I wondered if, after all, someone had seen something.

I SHOULD GIVE YOU a rundown on Luther Downing. He was tall, handsome, very black, with the body of a fine athlete, the jaw of a prize fighter, and the limpid dark eyes of a man who lived with some kind of sadness. He had a record of dozens of arrests during the Nixon administration for anti-war demonstrations. He had served six months in jail for leading a bussing riot in Boston. He had also won a Nobel prize for poetry and some sort of peace award from the Soviet government. He was, at the moment, giving a series of lectures in the Beaumont's Jefferson Room, and there had been demonstrations outside the hotel protesting his presence there by some hard-hat conservatives. I knew that Chambrun had been urged to refuse him accommodations and the use of the Jefferson Room and that Chambrun had told the urgers to drop dead.

Mrs. Kniffin had slipped away and Chambrun and Hardy and I waited for Downing to speak his piece.

He looked around the office, which is more like a handsome living room than a place of business. He looked at the painting on the wall that faced Chambrun's desk.

"A genuine Picasso, isn't it?" he asked. He had a voice like the low notes on an organ.

"A gift from the painter himself," Chambrun said.

Downing drew a deep breath. "Have you talked to the baby sitter?" he asked.

"What baby sitter?" Hardy asked.

"The one who was with the little girl last night," Downing said.

"She's off duty this morning," Chambrun said. "Should we have talked to her?"

"When you do," Downing said, "she will tell you that I had an encounter with the child last night."

The office was deathly still for a moment.

"Tell us about it, Mr. Downing," Hardy said.

I suddenly remembered Doc Partridge saying that Downing had been telling someone upstairs that he would be blamed. Because he was black.

"It must have been a little after eleven—last night," Downing said. "I was going out. Drinks with some friends across town." He flashed us a bitter, white smile. "I do have friends. When I came out of my room I saw the child standing outside the door of her suite. It's E, I think. She took a look at me, like she was suddenly excited. Then she came over to me— holding out her hand toward my face. I said hello, but she didn't say anything. Just came on till she was standing beside me. She made some kind of strange signal to me, and I suddenly realized she couldn't speak. Jesus! Deaf and dumb, I thought. Things like that make me sick at my stomach. I wanted to get out of there but she had hold of my sleeve. I—I kept talking, I don't know what the hell about, but she couldn't hear or understand. Then she reached up and touched my cheek, and her face lit up like a Christmas tree! Do you know what she was trying to tell me, man?''

''What?'' Hardy said very quietly.

''She was trying to tell me that my black face was beautiful, or at least that it pleased her.'' Downing suddenly shook himself, like a dog coming out of water. ''Goddamned kid had never heard anything about blacks, maybe never seen one up close before. She'd never heard anything about blacks that would frighten her or disgust her or turn her off. Because she couldn't hear! I tell you, you never had anything like that happen to you in your whole Christ-bitten life, because you aren't black! I—I bent down, and I touched her, and she kept stroking my cheek and indicating her pleasure. I was shook up real good, man.'' Downing's mouth turned into a straight, hard slit. ''Then this crazy broad came running down the hall, screaming at me. It seems she'd gone to borrow a portable TV set from the housekeeper. 'Take your hands off that child, you black bastard!' she shouted at me. The child didn't hear it, of course, and she kept smiling, trying to show the woman that she was pleased with me, that we were friends. I did a pretty fair job of controlling myself while I tried to explain to this woman what had happened. She just grabbed the child and pulled her back into Suite E.'' Again his chest swelled as he took a deep breath. ''That was last night.''

"There is more?" Hardy asked, his face expressionless.

"There is this morning," Downing said. There were little beads of sweat on his forehead and he wiped them away with a handkerchief. "Was she raped?"

"We don't have the Medical Examiner's report," Hardy said.

"An unofficial examination makes us think not," Chambrun said.

Hardy turned to look at Chambrun and I guessed he wouldn't have played it that way.

"I hope to God not," Downing said, "because some crazy sonofabitch will try to pin it on me. We blacks aren't supposed to be civilized when it comes to sex. And I hope to God not, because she was a nice little girl."

"About this morning," Hardy said. He had gone cold and hard.

Downing nodded slowly. "I saw her again," he said. "It was just about eleven-fifteen. I know because I had the eleven o'clock news on the radio in my room and the announcer was just signing off when someone knocked on my door. I went to see who it was, and there was the kid smiling up at me."

"She was alone? Did you see anyone else in the hall?" Hardy asked.

"No. There was no one."

"You didn't see a maid, or anyone connected with the hotel?"

"There was no one just then—when the kid stood outside my door, smiling at me."

"So you invited her in?" Hardy said. He sounded ominous. I think he thought a confession was coming.

"I did not. Not after that crazy woman the night before. I could see the headlines. 'Black Poet Charged with Molesting White Child.' There was all kinds of screaming and yelling going on down the hall. It was that French tart and her army of creeps. Of course the kid couldn't hear it."

"That must mean the door to Suite A or B was open. You couldn't hear screaming and yelling if the door wasn't open." Chambrun leaned forward in his chair. "Did anyone come out of A or B?"

"I didn't see anyone," Downing said. "I was trying with sign language to let the kid understand that I couldn't let her in. For Christ sake, she was trying to let me know that she was a friend, and I had to shut the door in her face. A black man can't run risks in a fancy whorehouse like this hotel."

"Perhaps I made a mistake giving you living room here," Chambrun said. You don't call the Beaumont a "whorehouse" and expect anything but anger from him.

"So you shut the door in the child's face," Hardy said.

Downing nodded. "I sent her away. If I hadn't, she might be alive."

"Which way did she go?"

"How the hell do I know? *I shut the door!* At the time I supposed she'd gone back to her suite."

Hardy studied him for a moment in silence. Then he said: "Thanks for coming in with your story. I'm going to ask you to repeat it to a police stenographer and sign it. You're sure about the time this morning?"

"I tell you, the news broadcast was just signing off. It was eleven-fifteen."

Downing left us. I felt a little frozen by the bitterness of a whole culture.

"The time is narrowed down," Chambrun said. He lit one of his flat Egyptian cigarettes and leaned back in his chair, his eyes narrowed. "Marilyn was at Downing's door at a quarter past eleven. Carol Failes started to look for her at eleven-thirty. At that time the doors to A or B or both were open. Downing heard them yelling at each other. I think we'd better bear down on Yvonne Darcel and Company."

"They all denied seeing the child," Hardy said.

"The murderer would certainly deny it," Chambrun said.

WE DIDN'T GET TO Yvonne Darcel and her friends right away. A call came from the lobby just as we were starting out. It was Johnny Thacker to tell Chambrun and Hardy that George Watson had just come back to the hotel and was headed for Fourteen. I remember looking at my watch. The ball game at Shea Stadium would not be over this soon. It wasn't quite four o'clock.

We went up to Fourteen. The place was crawling with Hardy's people. His number-one man, a Sergeant Fletcher, met us as we got off the elevator.

"I was coming to look for you, Lieutenant," Fletcher said. "The kid's father is back and he's staging some kind of a riot in E. I was trying to locate someone with a pass key.''

Chambrun stepped into the linen room and came out with a key with a large wooden tag on it. As we started down the corridor, the door to J opened and Mrs. Jasmine Velasquez Gilhooly saw us. Her red hair and the diamonds were almost blinding.

''Pierre!'' she said sharply.

Chambrun breezed past her and down the hall to E. Just as we got there, the door was opened and my gal Carol was ejected from the inside as if she'd been shot out of a cannon. Hardy caught her as she was about to fall on her face. Chambrun's reflexes were even faster. He managed to keep the door from being closed from the inside. Watson, trying to push him away, was shouting obscenities at him. Hardy, you might say, handed me Carol and added his weight to Chambrun's at the door. Watson took a swing at him and Hardy knocked him cold.

I had my arms around a sobbing Carol. ''He's trying to kill her,'' she managed to tell me.

We went into E, Hardy dragging Watson along the floor by the back of his coat collar. Carol broke away from me and ran to Helen Watson, who was standing in the middle of the living room.

I don't know what was keeping her on her feet. Her mouth was bruised and bleeding, one eye was almost swollen shut. Her jaw looked a little lopsided. She spoke, and it was thick-sounding, almost unintelligible.

"When I told him what—what had happened to Marilyn he—he went crazy," she said. "Is he hurt?" She sounded curious, not concerned.

"Get Dr. Partridge up here on the double," Chambrun said to me.

"Oh, that won't be necessary, Mr. Chambrun," Helen Watson said, and, unbelievably, she laughed. It was a short, mirthless little laugh. "This is nothing new. It's one of the ways George demonstrates his maleness."

"I'll remember that, you bitch!"

George Watson was coming to. He had pulled himself up on his hands and knees and was staring balefully at his wife. Hardy held out his hand and helped to pull Watson up to his feet.

"Sorry, but you didn't leave me much choice," the big detective said.

"I won't forget," Watson said. He turned his attention to Chambrun. He was touching his jaw tenderly. Hardy's fist must have felt like a sledgehammer. "Now, Mr. Chambrun, would you mind telling me exactly what's happened here. My wife tells me—"

"Your daughter wandered out of here while Mrs. Watson and Miss Failes were looking at clothes in the bedroom. Marilyn spoke to Mr. Downing across the hall at a quarter past eleven. At eleven-thirty—"

"Marilyn didn't speak to anyone as you damn well know!" Watson said. Anger made his voice shake.

"She had a way of speaking, George, as you damn well know," Helen Watson said.

"You keep your mouth shut!" Watson shouted at her. "You were so anxious to get yourself gussied up for your boy friend you forgot all about her. Well, you can go wallow in the hay with him because I have no reason to spend another five minutes of my life with you. But before I take off I want Mr. Chambrun to tell me how this could have happened in his hotel. Incidentally, Chambrun, I'm going to sue you out of your drawers for having your boy here assault me."

"My 'boy here,'" Chambrun said, ice cold, "is Lieutenant Hardy of Homicide, investigating the murder."

"With a few questions for you, Mr. Watson," Hardy said. "I understand you were at Brooks Brothers this morning buying clothes. That you then went to Shea Stadium to a ball game."

"That was the schedule," Watson said. "Mr. Haskell runs my life for me on this goddamned trip." He gave me a dirty look.

"But you didn't go to Brooks Brothers," Hardy said. "They were expecting you, but you never put in an appearance. I had you paged at Shea Stadium when the murder was discovered. You didn't respond to the paging and you weren't in the Beaumont's box where you were supposed to be."

"So I didn't want the goddamned clothes and I didn't go to the goddamned ball game. Is there any law against that?"

"Where were you between eleven and eleven-thirty this morning?" Hardy asked.

Watson's face turned scarlet with rage. "Are you suggesting I might have murdered my own kid?"

"Having seen you in action, it's a fair question," Hardy said.

"Why, you low-grade sonofabitch!" Watson shouted.

Hardy turned to Fletcher, who was standing in the doorway. "Take Mr. Watson down to the first floor office, Sergeant. I'll talk to him when he's cooled off a little."

"I'm not going anywhere till you bastards tell me exactly what—"

"Put handcuffs on him if it's necessary, Sergeant," Hardy said. He looked at Watson. "I suggest you go quietly, Mr. Watson, or I'll have you taken out of here on a stretcher."

Hardy had obviously been doing his usual careful homework. Watson decided it was the better part of valor to go quietly with Fletcher. As soon as he was gone, Helen Watson moved unsteadily toward the couch and sat down.

I have seen people before who have been crushed by tragedy. Very often there are no tears, no visible emotions, only a stony control. Later, sometimes much later, the dam breaks. Helen Watson sat there on the couch, looking from one to the other of us with glazed eyes. Carol Failes was clinging to me as if she needed that support to hold her up. She seemed nearer to coming apart than Helen.

"He came in here and she told him what had happened and he—he just started beating on her," Carol said in something like a whisper. "When I tried to interfere, he—he threw me out into the hall. Thank God you were there or he might have killed her."

"Oh, no, he wouldn't have killed me," Helen said, matter-of-fact. "He needs me. He needs someone to blame for everything. You see, Marilyn is my fault. Marilyn is responsible for his failures, so I am responsible for his failures. He needs me to get even with the world.''

"My God!'' Carol said, and clung tighter to me.

"You're wondering about the lover he mentioned, the lover I'm supposed to have,'' Helen said.

"The man in the Blue Lagoon last night?'' Chambrun asked.

She nodded slowly, methodically. "Herbert North,'' she said. "He's a home town boy—Carlton's Creek. I was in love with him when I was sixteen and in high school. I took it for granted that someday Herb and I would be married. But then—'' She hesitated, looked down at her hands which rested, motionless, in her lap. "Then Herb went away to college and I—I dated George. He was the glamor boy at the high school, captain of the football team, star of the baseball team. Most likely to succeed, president of the senior class. One night we went to a sort of night spot where there was music and dancing. I let myself be persuaded to have a couple of drinks. And then—then, because I was full of sexual desires that had never been satisfied, I let George make love to me. I was sick with shame and guilt afterwards—and pregnant.'' She drew a deep, shuddering breath and I thought she might be going to come apart then, but she didn't. She went on in the same level voice. "Abortion was unheard-of and unattainable in Carlton's Creek. When it became impossible to hide the fact that I was pregnant, George, reluctantly, asked me to marry him, and I, reluctantly, accepted. I was still in love with Herb North and sick with the hurt I'd done him. I didn't see him again for a long time. He went into the Marines and was three years in Vietnam. Meanwhile, Marilyn was born.'' She paused for a long time and it occurred to me that no one was breathing, the room was so still. ''It was almost a year before we knew for certain that she would never hear or speak. 'A deaf and dummy' George called her. He hated me for it because he thought it brought shame on him. What really brought shame on him was that he couldn't control his temper, couldn't hold a job, couldn't bear to start at the bottom. He was 'most likely to succeed.' He had been the irresistible glamor boy, and to prove that he still was he began to have affairs with every available unhappy woman in Carlton's Creek. That was when he began manhandling and beating me—as though he was God's instrument for punishing me for Marilyn.''

''Why didn't you leave him?'' Carol burst out.

''He expressed loathing and contempt for Marilyn in private, but when he was with her he was kind and gentle. The only time I ever saw him like that. And he was her father. And I, God help me, felt guilty. Maybe I was at fault in some way. We talked about separating quite often. He refused—on Marilyn's account. I think the real reason was that being married and with a handicapped child none of his other women could reasonably make demands on him. That's the way it is.''

''And Herbert North?'' I heard myself ask her.

''Herbert came back from Vietnam. Carlton's Creek was buzzing with talk about George and me. He knew the marriage was a disaster. He came to see me one day when George was at work. He told me he still loved me, he would take me away, he would care for Marilyn. In the middle of that George came home. He'd been fired again. Herb laid it on the line to George and George beat him half to death. He was in the hospital for almost a month. He refused to bring charges against George, I think because he knew George would tell the whole world that Herb and I were having a thing together. People would have believed it." Again there was a long silence. "That was eight years ago. I never saw Herb again until last night, when he turned up in the Blue Lagoon with his sister. You probably know George took off after he'd confronted Herb. Until this horror of Marilyn this morning I've been terrified that George had tracked Herb down and attacked him again."

"Do you know where North is staying?" Hardy asked.

"No. I just saw him across the room. I had no words with him."

"You don't know where your husband has spent his time today, Mrs. Watson?"

"No."

"Or have a guess?"

She spread her hands in a little gesture of despair. "We don't have any friends in New York." Her mouth twitched at its corners and I thought perhaps the breakdown was coming. "We don't have any friends, period."

Chambrun moved into the picture. "Did you know that Marilyn had made a friend here on Fourteen?"

She looked puzzled. "A friend?"

"A man living down the hall in C."

Her eyes widened and she lifted her hands to her mouth. "The *black* man?"

"He's a poet of some distinction," Chambrun said.

"The woman who baby-sat for us told me that man was making some sort of advances to Marilyn. I never dreamed! Do you mean—"

"I mean Miss Gault, who was your sitter, is a conclusion jumper," Chambrun said. He sounded irritated. "Luther Downing has helped us narrow down some of our time problems, Mrs. Watson. It seems Marilyn went to see him this morning when she wandered away from here. Your daughter didn't seem to know that there was anything odd about being black, and he had been friendly. Importantly, he knows that it was exactly eleven-fifteen when she knocked on his door. When did you realize Marilyn was gone?"

Carol answered his question. "It was eleven-thirty, Mr. Chambrun. Helen was trying on a dress. She asked me to look in here—the living room—to see if Marilyn was all right. She was gone somewhere."

"We weren't terribly worried," Helen said. "But Carol insisted on calling Mr. Haskell to ask him if the hotel security people would keep an eye open for her."

"So whatever happened to her took place in a span of no more than fifteen minutes," Chambrun said.

"I think we'd better talk to the French crowd who were running in and out of their suites," Hardy said.

I HAD HAD OCCASION take notice of Mlle. Yvonne Darcel with a rather natural masculine interest. She was dark, with very bright blue eyes shaded by very long black lashes that I thought were really her own. She was an artist at makeup, not too much and expertly applied. She seemed to be always in motion. She spoke English very fluently, very rapidly, and with an intriguing accent. She illustrated everything she said with dramatic gestures, her hands tapering and beautifully cared for. She used a perfume that you were aware of yards away, but for her it was in good taste. Everything about her spelled sex in capital letters.

We left a shaky Carol with Helen Watson, but we didn't get to Mlle. Darcel as quickly as we wanted. The news of Chambrun's presence on Fourteen had spread and the moment we stepped out of the E suite we were surrounded. The Arab in his burnoose was there. He was due to make a speech at the United Nations in half an hour. We couldn't hold him there. He had diplomatic immunity as far as the police were concerned. The quadruplets, looking like four earnest, bespectacled college professors, had to get downstairs for the afternoon round of the bridge championship. If they were forced to default, it would destroy their chances of winning. It would be an international disaster.

The Greek billionaire, grim yet smiling, his bodyguard at his side, made it very clear he had the power and the money to put the Beaumont out of business if he was interfered with any further. He was dark, suntanned to a mahogany color, probably from standing on the bridge of his yacht, and the bodyguard, with a flowing mustache, looked like a villain out of *Arabian Nights*.

Hardy made it clear everyone would have to stay put till he had statements from them. They all demanded that they be first.

As we approached Suites A and B, occupied by the French troupe, there was Mrs. Jasmine Velasquez Gilhooly standing opposite in the doorway to J.

"Pierre, I must talk to you," she said.

Chambrun bowed elegantly over her hand, kissed it, and promised he would join her as quickly as he could.

"It is important," she said.

"Anything you have to say is important to me, Jasmine," he said. "But in a little while."

One thing was certain. The doors to both A and B were open and Mrs. Gilhooly had a right to complain. What was going on inside sounded like a free-for-all in the animal cage at the zoo.

We went in because nobody answered Chambrun's knock. It looked like the stage-set for a Feydeau farce in there. Yvonne Darcel was wearing a black negligee, cut down to there, her luscious breasts looking ready to pop out at any instant. She and her husband, Paul Martine, who looked like a sleek headwaiter in a smart restaurant, were screaming at each other in French. The secretary and double, Marie Orell, wearing a smart pink linen summer suit, was enough like Yvonne to be her twin. She was looking at the quarrelers with a faint smile of contempt. Lounging in an armchair right by Marie was a lean, blond Englishman with a military mustache, reported to be Yvonne's lover. His name was Charles "Chip" Nelson. Chip Nelson drove racing cars when he wasn't otherwise involved. Right now he was involved in gently caressing Marie Orell's thigh. I wondered if he couldn't tell the two women apart. Mlle. Orell didn't seem to mind. In the background were two maids, right out of Feydeau. They wore little black dresses that came about halfway down their thighs, black stockings, little white aprons and white caps. They looked at each other, then away at the quarrelers, then back at each other like manipulated puppets.

Yvonne Darcel caught sight of Chambrun, turned on him, and launched into a torrent of French, her voice rising and falling like some off-key musical instrument. She was angry beyond belief. I speak a little French, but I couldn't follow a single sentence of the torrent she was unleashing at Chambrun.

He listened for a moment and then held up a hand to silence her. "I think it would be better if we spoke English, ma'amselle," he said. "This is Lieutenant Hardy of the New York police. You know Mark Haskell."

She gave me such a dazzling smile that I dreamed for a moment that I'd been on her mind.

"Do you always leave the hall doors to your suite open, Miss Darcel?" Hardy asked.

She went off again into a screaming flow of French.

"The lady suffers from claustrophobia," Chambrun said. He was fighting a smile. "She feels 'shut in' when the doors are closed."

"That may be very lucky for us," Hardy said. "You know why we're here, Miss Darcel?"

Again a flood of French.

"English please," Chambrun said.

"That miserable little house detective told us," Yvonne said. "What could we possibly know about the child?"

I got the picture then. The preliminary questioning had been done by Jerry Dodd, our man. He is never called a "house detective." He is the "security officer."

"The child had to go by your open doors to get to where she was found," Hardy said. "Alone or with someone."

"I assure you, none of us saw the child, Lieutenant," Paul Martine said, as polite as though Hardy had been a cherished guest in that mythical restaurant. The two little maids bounced and squeaked at us in French. I could understand them well enough to know that they were swearing, on their mothers' graves, that they had never seen Marilyn.

Marie Orell, who had moved a little closer to the armchair to facilitate Chip Nelson's stroking, asked when they were supposed to have seen the child.

"Between eleven-fifteen and eleven-thirty," Hardy told her.

"Ah, well, then I couldn't have seen her," the lady said. "I was in my bedroom at the rear of Suite B, dressing."

"I hadn't even waked up yet," Chip Nelson said. "Sorry, no help, I'm afraid."

"But you were up and around, Miss Darcel," Hardy said.

"Eleven-thirty is very early in the morning for me," Yvonne said.

"Not too early for you to have sent for the house-keeper to complain about the supply of towels in Suite B," Hardy said.

"Ah, yes, that," Yvonne said.

"So you were up and about at the critical time," Hardy said. "I assume that, because of your claustrophobia, the suite doors were open."

"They may have been," Yvonne said.

"They were, ma'amselle," Chambrun said. "Mrs. Gilhooly, across the hall, was complaining about the noisy quarreling."

"We were not quarreling," Paul Martine said. "I wasn't even up."

"But Mrs. Martine was," Hardy said. "Perhaps she was shouting at the housekeeper."

"I do not like to be called Martine," Yvonne said. "I am Yvonne Darcel."

"Whatever you like, Miss Darcel," Hardy said. He was losing patience. "But you were up and around and yelling at someone, the hall doors of your two suites open, at the precise moment that little Marilyn Watson, alone or with someone, passed by. I ask you to remember."

She looked at Hardy with an exaggerated pity. He, obviously to her, was not very bright. "My dear Lieutenant," she said, "people look at me, I do not look at people."

Charles Chip Nelson guffawed. "Oh, my, Yvonne, that's very good, very good indeed!" He continued to stroke Miss Orell's thigh.

This, I told myself, was a madhouse.

"It is essential that we be permitted to go out," Paul Martine said. "There is a special screening of Yvonne's new film. For her not to be there would be very bad public relations. We are already late."

"I, too, am late," Hardy said, "and it would be even worse public relations for Miss Darcel if she refuses to cooperate."

Yvonne waved her arms in a gesture of despair. "Shall I spell it out for you, word by word, Lieutenant? I never saw the child. Maybe she was there, but I never saw her. Why should I notice a twelve-year-old child wandering around the halls?"

"Because she was on the way to being murdered," Hardy said. He was fed-up. "Knowing that, I could hope your memory might be restored."

For the moment it was a losing game for Hardy. Chambrun took a hand.

"The Lieutenant is going to want written statements from all of you," he said. "The sooner that is done, the sooner you will all be free to go about your business. Meanwhile—" He beckoned to me and we walked out in the hall, leaving Hardy to get his statements.

"I would like you to stay with me while I talk to Mrs. Gilhooly," Chambrun said.

I grinned at him. "You afraid of her?"

"I'm not in the mood for nostalgia," he said.

I SUSPECT that Jasmine Velasquez Gilhooly was a sentimental slob behind her rather tough, hard-boiled exterior. It seems that Sebastian Velasquez, a member of the Spanish royal family, had first seen Jasmine playing peek-a-boo with a cheering male audience in the old Columbia burlesque theater on Broadway. He had courted her, married her, and introduced her to her first taste of real luxury by buying her a honeymoon at the Beaumont. Velasquez, with no particular design in mind, had been assigned to 14J for that memorable occasion. J for Jasmine had been pure coincidence.

That was B.C.—before Chambrun, who was fighting the Nazis in the back alleys of Paris.

Velasquez lasted for about five years. They say that was all his royal heart could take in the athletic sex world of Jasmine. He left her with money in the millions and she promptly crossed oceans to mourn him at the Beaumont—in 14J. That's the first sign of sentimental slobism.

By then the Beaumont had a new manager, one Pierre Chambrun, dashing hero of the French Resistance. The fact that she was fifteen years older than Chambrun didn't deter Jasmine Velasquez. According to Chambrun she did the courting, and I suspect the age difference didn't bother him, since he was not interested in permanence. Jasmine in her mid forties was still a very exciting and appetizing dish. But, when it became apparent that Chambrun's answer was a definite "no," being a good loser, Jasmine, without recriminations, went hunting elsewhere. I'm not clear about where she discovered Francis Xavier Gilhooly. F.X. Gilhooly had risen from a brawling, hard-drinking hod carrier to an international king of finance. He had started his climb as an independent constructor of outhouses, and gone on to become a contractor for modest homes, then office buildings, then railroad depots and world fairs, then skyscrapers in New York, London, and Paris. I don't know if he was aware of any significance to his honeymoon with Jasmine in Suite 14J at the Beaumont. She had honeymooned there before, in that same king-sized double bed. She was showing Chambrun that she had, handsomely, survived his turn-down. Sentiment and showing the world!

As age approached, F.X. Gilhooly decided that every couple of retirement age should have a simple little $100,000 condominium. He built them all over the world and he left a vast empire to Jasmine when she outlasted him on a warm summer night. As I have said, what a way to go.

And now, thirty years after Chambrun's "no," she had waited two weeks to bed herself down once more in 14J.

She was waiting in the open door of 14J when Chambrun and I emerged from the French madhouse in A and B.

"It's depressing to realize that I have lost my hold over you, Pierre," she said. Her eyes were dancing, surrounded by crow's-feet etched there by laughter.

"Only severe trouble would have delayed me, Jasmine," he said.

Her eyes clouded. "Poor tragic little kid," she said. We went into her suite and she closed the door, shutting out the jabbering French contingent. "I didn't ask you to come here to complain about the noise, Pierre, though God knows it is a matter for complaint." She smiled at me. "You missed a very good martini, young man."

"Regrets," I said. "I had the same troubles as Mr. Chambrun."

There were bottles of bourbon, Scotch, and vodka, an ice bucket, and glasses on the coffee table in front of the couch. She sat down on the couch and gestured to them. She crossed her legs. They were still remarkably good legs. We both said no to a drink.

"I may be wasting your time, Pierre. You generally know what other people know before they know it themselves." She put ice in an old fashioned glass and filled it with vodka. I wondered if that was her idea of a nice, dry martini. "That child haunts me," she said.

"You saw her today?" Chambrun asked.

"No. Last night. I was just coming in from the theater. Some ghastly modern thing about a little boy who blinds horses, with a nude scene thrown in for good measure."

Chambrun smiled. "Nude scenes used to be your specialty," he said.

"In my day we took off our clothes to please, not to shock," Jasmine said. "The child's mother was discussing something with someone I took to be a baby sitter. The child saw me and came down the hall. She pointed at my hair. It took me a moment to realize she couldn't hear or speak. But I understood she was asking me a question. Was my hair real?" The bright henna red was obviously not real. "Oh, it's real, Pierre, in the sense that it isn't a wig. Let me see, was it blonde in the days I was chasing you?"

"It was what gentlemen prefer," he said.

"Or was it chestnut red that year?" She smiled at him, and then the smile faded. "The child was so eager, so curious, and yet unable to get answers to her questions. The mother came down the hall, apologized. There was no reason for an apology."

"But you didn't see her again today?"

"No. Really, Pierre, you better let me tell you what's on my mind, even if you already know it. In Suite I, next door, there is a man. Do you know him, Pierre?"

"Henry Bowers," Chambrun said. "No, I don't know him."

"How does he rate a suite on Fourteen if you don't know him?"

Chambrun frowned. "By special request of the State Department," he said.

"God save us all from diplomacy. It is the disease of sophisticated children. You don't know why the State Department wants him here?"

"'Mine not to reason why—'" Chambrun said.

"I have encountered this man at another time," Jasmine said. "His name wasn't Henry Bowers then. I suspect he has many names."

"Why are you interested in him?" Chambrun asked.

She swallowed half of her vodka and put the glass down. "Because he is a professional killer," she said. "Did you know that, Pierre?"

Chambrun's eyes narrowed, and there was an angry glitter in them. "What possible interest could a professional killer have in a little girl from Carlton's Creek?"

"No notion," Jasmine said. She took a cigarette out of a box on the table and lit it. "Men are peculiar creatures," she said after she had exhaled a cloud of smoke. "They have different kinds of sexual quirks— but they are all quirkish."

"And Mr. Bowers' quirk is—?"

"I haven't the faintest idea," Jasmine said. "I was thinking of F.X." She glanced at me. "Francis Xavier Gilhooly, my late husband."

"Let's stay with Mr. Bowers," Chambrun said.

"I am staying with him. It was F.X. who told me who he was. It was F.X.'s particular sexual quirk that got me involved some twenty years ago with this man who calls himself Bowers. His name was Fritz Kuglemann in those days, supposedly German. F.X. enjoyed having me flirt with other men; sometimes go even further than a flirtation. My whole life has been involved with pleasing men—with only one notable failure." She blinked her eyes at Chambrun. "F.X.'s quirk was that he enjoyed getting me back. I would join him after I'd spent time with someone else, and he would tear off my clothes, shouting that he was the greatest in the world and nobody could steal me from him. Then he would make love to me as only an Irish bricklayer can, no techniques, no games, just good old-time passion. He was marvelous in bed."

Chambrun's face had gone rock-hard. "Are you telling me that you had an affair with this man Bowers?" he asked.

"I was on the way to it," Jasmine said matter-of-factly. "But this time F.X. called me off. 'Stay away from Kuglemann,' he told me. 'He is a professional killer and assassin. Involve us with him and God knows who the consequences might be.' So I backed away.''

"And that's it?''

"That was twenty years ago. F.X. was building an airport in Romania in those days.''

"For the Russians?''

Jasmine shrugged. "Their money is money,'' she said. "F.X. thought Kuglemann might be an agent for West Germany at the time.''

"I still don't tie that in to a little girl from Carlton's Creek,'' Chambrun said.

Jasmine was obviously going to tell her story her way. "Five years ago I was in Cairo grieving for F.X., who had died six months before. I was in a café with a nice old British diplomat who was long past anything more than remembering how good he had been in his youth. There was a party of Egyptian hot-shots at a corner table. Suddenly there was an explosion near the bar. It broke bottles and glasses, ripped the arm off a very nice young man who was the assistant bartender.'' She was so casual about it she could have been describing a traffic tie-up in Times Square. "In the excitement, with everyone screaming and yelling and trying to find a way out—people always think there will be a second bomb when there has been a first one—I saw a man approach the table where the Egyptian hot-shots seemed to be kind of frozen. He was holding a napkin up to his face. I saw the gun he was holding. He shot one of the Egyptians three times, blowing off the top of his head. Then he ran. Somebody made a grab at him and pulled away the napkin with which he was covering his face. I recognized him.''

''Kuglemann?'' Chambrun asked.

''Or Henry Bowers, or whatever he chooses to call himself,'' Jasmine said. ''Well, yesterday I ran into this man in the corridor out there. He looked straight through me as though I wasn't there. But I wondered—''

''If you had seen him once too often?'' Chambrun asked, his voice cold and hard.

''I thought I'd better tell you as soon as I could, Pierre. There was a chance I might be too dead to do it later.''

IN THE EARLY GOING the only people missing from Fourteen were George Watson and the State Department's Mr. Bowers. George had come back, but Bowers was still among the missing. Chambrun tried to call him on the phone from Jasmine's rooms. No answer. Then we went down the hall, rang the doorbell for 14I without results. Chambrun let us in with his pass key.

Bowers, or Kuglemann, or whoever, was traveling light. There was one airplane-luggage bag in his closet and one rumpled gray suit hanging there. There were two clean shirts and a soiled one in a bureau drawer. A set of underwear was hanging on the shower curtain in the bathroom. Bowers evidently did his own laundry. There was a shaving kit and a toothbrush and paste. There was one clean handkerchief in the top bureau drawer along with a bottle of aspirin tablets. There was nothing else; no letters, no piece of paper of any sort, no note or appointment scribbled on the telephone pad. From searching his room Bowers was a zero, except that he was far too modestly equipped for an occupant of a suite at the Beaumont.

Chambrun was in a dark mood. As we left Bowers' suite, we saw the four scholarly bridge players heading for the elevators. They'd evidently made their statements and been released by Hardy. All was quiet in the Darcel suites.

Back in Chambrun's office Miss Ruysdale was on the job again, though Miss Simmons was still handling the phones. Ruysdale was in Chambrun's private room along with Jerry Dodd, our security man. Jerry's lean, pointed face looked smudged with fatigue. Though these two were, with me, the closest people to Chambrun on the staff, the great man walked over to his desk without a word of greeting. Miss Ruysdale produced a cup of Turkish coffee from the sideboard.

"You will please put through a person-to person call to Wallace Sandberg at the State Department in Washington," Chambrun said, and Miss Ruysdale evaporated into the outer office. He lifted his heavy lids to look at Jerry. "Well?" he said.

"A blank," Jerry said. "No one on the staff saw the Watson kid this morning. No one saw any unexplained characters wandering around. No weapon has turned up anywhere. Hardy, as you know, is questioning the guests on Fourteen. So far nothing."

"Not quite nothing, as you will hear when I get my phone call," Chambrun said.

"You go over it and over it and come up empty-handed each time," Jerry said. "The Medical Examiner has removed the most likely motive. No sexual assault. That does away with the idea of some depraved kook hiding behind a respectable identity. Somebody just beat the child to death with the proverbial 'blunt instrument.' Why, for God sake?''

"She saw something she wasn't supposed to see," Chambrun said. He sipped at his coffee. "She was curious, unafraid. She made contact with at least two people on the floor last night—Luther Downing and Mrs. Gilhooly. She tried to make contact again this morning with Downing. That was at exactly eleven-fifteen. Mrs. Watson and Carol Failes missed her and started looking for her at eleven-thirty. That narrows down the time for us.''

"But what could she have seen?" Jerry asked.

"Something pretty extraordinary that made it necessary to silence her.''

"She was already silenced—by way of God," Jerry said.

"But she could communicate. Maybe she could have acted out what she saw. It must have happened so suddenly the killer didn't take time to discover that she couldn't hear or speak." Chambrun twisted in his chair. "Maybe the killer thought she heard something, not knowing that she was stone-deaf.''

"Jesus!" Jerry said.

Ruysdale appeared in the doorway and pointed to Chambrun's phone. He beckoned to her to come in and switched on the squawk box on his desk so that we could all hear the conversation.

"Wallace?" he said.

Wallace Sandberg's voice was cheerful and hearty. "Pierre, nice to hear from you. And thanks for taking care of our man Bowers."

"You're not welcome," Chambrun said. "I have just learned this afternoon that your man Bowers is a killer, a hit man, an assassin."

"Oh, now wait a minute, Pierre—"

"We've had a murder here in the hotel," Chambrun said. "A twelve-year-old child, a girl. She had a suite across the hall from Bowers. She was, unhappily, a deaf mute. But someone thought she had seen or heard something that had to be kept a secret."

"Not Bowers," Sandberg said.

"Or Kuglemann, or whatever his real name is. He's at the top of my list, Wallace, and I'm about to land on him hard if he hasn't already taken a powder."

"You've got it all wrong, Pierre."

"I know that he shot an Egyptian big-shot to death in a Cairo café five years ago," Chambrun said. "That's enough for me."

"How do you know that?"

"If I told you, somebody else might be killed."

"Now listen to me, Pierre." Sandberg's voice sounded strangled. "I can't tell you why Bowers is staying at your hotel. But I can tell you that he is a trusted operative for us."

"Can anyone trust your assurances?"

"For God sake, Pierre! Let me tell you there is no reason in the world why Bowers should kill your little girl. He's there to watch and report. That's all."

"Who is he watching?"

"I'm sorry, Pierre."

"I'm sorry, too," Chambrun said. His anger was controlled, but I knew it was at a boiling level. "He's going to have to do his watching somewhere else. Could be from the city jail. If you've asked me to accommodate a murderer, you've gone too far, Wallace. That goes for now and for the future."

He reached out and switched off the squawker. "I want that man, Jerry, the minute he sets foot in the hotel—if he sets foot."

"He doesn't know you suspect him," Jerry said. "He'll come back for his things."

"There isn't fifty dollars' worth of stuff in his room," Chambrun said. "He doesn't have to come back for anything if he wants to avoid Hardy's questions. But I want him, Jerry. I want him very badly. That was a nice little girl; too nice to have this happen to her. I want everything on him. Who saw him leave the hotel? When? What he had for breakfast and what time? Phone calls he made. I want the works on Mr. Henry Bowers."

"Consider it done," Jerry said.

It is CHAMBRUN'S HABIT to remind me, in moments of crisis, that we "still have a hotel to run." I have known people in my time who, like circus jugglers, could keep half a dozen balls in the air at the same time. Chambrun made them look like amateurs. He could keep dozens and dozens of balls in the air and never—or almost never—miss. He considered a violence in the hotel a miss. Anything that disrupted the perpetual perfection of the operation was a miss. When there was a "miss," Chambrun became a kind of grim avenger. He was driven by fiends until the culprit was caught and duly punished.

But we still had a hotel to run.

I was not a detective, professional or amateur, so I got the high sign from Chambrun the minute he terminated his dialogue with the man in the State Department. One of our busy times was coming up. I should check the machinery.

Three times each day there is an influx of nonresident patrons: lunchtime, the cocktail hour about five, and the after-theater crowd in the Blue Lagoon. The cocktail hour was almost on us when I left Chambrun.

The truth is that I become nearer to being "mien host" at the Beaumont than the great man himself. At the busy times I wander from busy place to busy place, covering the main dining room and the grill at lunch, the Trapeze Bar which hangs like a giant bird cage over the lobby, the Spartan Bar, where elderly males play backgammon and chess and even gin rummy and reminisce about the good old days of Calvin Coolidge and Herbert Hoover and dream that someday that bright young man, Ronald Reagan, will restore some kind of sanity to our way of life. I smile and nod to people, stop to chat with someone occasionally or when I am summoned. But primarily I am studying the workings of the machinery, trying to sense, with something approaching Chambrun's skill, that something in the atmosphere that suggests there is a hitch somewhere, a malfunction. I don't ever expect to acquire Chambrun's expertise, but I'm not bad at the job.

As I have mentioned, the Trapeze Bar is suspended over the lobby. It gets its name from a collection of little plastic figures, circus acrobats, designed by some forgotten friend of Chambrun's. The carefully circulated air in the room keeps the little figures on their trapezes in constant motion.

I went directly to the Trapeze from Chambrun's office. The place was already crowded with people talking, laughing, and drinking. Mr. Del Greco, the Trapeze's suave maître d', flagged me at the entrance.

"If you're ducking the press, Mr. Haskell, you'd better go somewhere else," he said.

"Who?" I said.

"Mike Traynor. He's been asking for you. Had me call your office."

There was no way I could avoid Mike sooner or later, so I thought it might better be sooner. I looked around and saw him grinning at me from a corner table. He's dark, with a homely, smiling face that has the map of Ireland printed all over it. I have always played ball with Mike and in return he's never blown anything I've told him in confidence. I told Del Greco to send my usual, a double Jack Daniel's on the rocks, to Mike's table.

"I was just about to give up on you, chum," Mike said when I joined him.

"Rough day," I said.

"I can imagine," he said. He waited.

"I can't tell you much that you don't already know," I said.

"Little girl clubbed to death, jammed in a trash barrel. That's what I know. Since I don't have to make a morning deadline, I decided to be patient. No story is just as good as half a story.''

Mike works for *Newsview*, the weekly news magazine. His deadline was Monday morning, four days away.

"So far there isn't any kind of a lead," I told him. "The child, Marilyn Watson, whose parents—"

"I've done my legwork," Mike interrupted.

"Marilyn was alive and well at eleven-fifteen. At eleven-thirty she was missing and a search was started for her. You see, she was—"

"—deaf and dumb," Mike said.

"No one admits to having seen her after eleven-fifteen. She wasn't found till around one-thirty. Her head was beaten to a pulp, but she wasn't sexually molested."

"Lovely phrase that, sexually molested. 'Please, my love, may I sexually molest you?' What garbage the formal police language is. So why was she killed?"

"We haven't a clue. Chambrun thinks she saw something, or someone believed she had heard something."

"But she couldn't hear."

"The murderer didn't stop to ask her that, or threaten her. He just killed her—boom!"

"The lucky Watsons. I was supposed to do a story on them." Mike's smile had faded.

The waiter brought my drink. As I took a swallow, I realized I hadn't had anything to eat or drink since breakfast.

"Why have you been ducking me?" Mike asked. "You must be holding something back."

"I haven't been ducking. It began with looking for the child, and when she'd been found, with questioning the staff, the other guests on Fourteen. I can give you a list of those guests, if you want it."

"I've already got it, chum," Mike said. "Everybody had a familiar sound except someone named Bowers."

I hesitated and Mike's expectant grin returned.

"Off the record for the moment," I said.

"If you say so and will tell me why."

"He's some kind of operator for the State Department. They asked us to take him in and locate him on Fourteen. He's watching someone."

"Who?"

"We haven't been told. The State Department wouldn't like it if we blew his cover. Not yet, anyway."

"Screw the State Department I always say," Mike said. "Well, we can assume—and regret—he wasn't watching the Watsons. If they were being watched, it would be by Internal Revenue. Those four kooky bridge players don't add up. No one watches Yvonne Darcel except people who want to 'sexually molest' her. Chambrun's old girl friend is past her prime. That leaves the Greek Midas and the Shah of Persia, or whoever Abdel Ghorra is, and the black poet. I put my money on him."

"Why, for God sake?" I asked.

"Luther Downing was against the war in Vietnam," Mike said. "He led a lot of demonstrations against the war and went to jail for some of them. That puts him on the State Department's enemy list—

along with a hundred million other Americans." Mike,
I saw, was quite serious.

At that moment I saw Mr. Del Greco almost running between the tables towards us.

"You're wanted in the lobby," he told me.

"Why?" I asked.

"There's been a shooting," he said. "Someone
killed outside the Fifth Avenue entrance."

"Who?"

Del Greco shrugged. He didn't know.

The lobby was in a turmoil when Mike and I got
there, people shouting and yelling at each other,
crowding toward the Fifth Avenue entrance. Mike and
I wedged our way through people and went out the
revolving door to the sidewalk. There was a crowd
there surrounding Waters, the doorman, and a body
stretched out on the pavement, covered by Waters'
uniform jacket. Waters was clutching his left shoulder and I could see blood trickling through his fingers.

"What the hell happened?" I asked Waters.

His face was twisted with pain and about thirty-five
people tried to tell me, all talking at once. I concen-
trated on Waters.

"Someone in a car opened fire," he said. "I was hit,
and this other guy was riddled. It sounded like a machine pistol."

I turned and found myself opposite a stone-faced
Chambrun. He bent down and pulled back the uniform jacket that was covering the dead man. I felt my
heart jam against my ribs.

Luther Downing's wide brown eyes stared up at the sky in death. Mike Traynor had hold of my arm. It jolted him, too. We'd just been talking about Downing.

I remember thinking that, sure as God, the black poet had been on somebody's enemy list.

PART TWO

ONE

THE FOURTEENTH FLOOR at the Beaumont was not a lucky place to live that day. There was nothing in the world to tie together the bludgeoning of Marilyn Watson and the sidewalk assassination of Luther Downing in my mind except that they were living on Fourteen. There was the coincidence that these two unlucky people had been involved in a wordless contact with each other.

One thing was quite certain. The Beaumont was going to be center stage in a very unwelcome spotlight. I was going to have to try to soften the glare of that exposure.

My problem wasn't made easier by the fact that we had been invaded earlier by a small army of photographers. They were on hand to get some sort of picture story of the fortunate Watsons from Carlton's Creek, and had stayed on when the disappearance and murder of Marilyn presented them with new and uglier subject matter. In addition there had been a couple of television cameramen out on the street, covering the demonstrators against the presence of Luther Downing in the hotel. Both cameramen had gotten partial pictures of the hit on Downing. There was hope they had gotten enough to nail a killer when their films were processed.

The presence of Hardy and his crew in the hotel meant that it was only a matter of minutes between the shooting and a complete takeover by the police. There had been fifty or sixty demonstrators outside the hotel, all carrying placards bearing somewhat the same message: The Beaumont was housing a Communist plotter who was bent on destroying our liberties. This all sprang from some kind of an encounter between Downing and one of the construction unions. Downing had claimed that the construction workers were discriminating against blacks and he had led a demonstration outside some office building that was rising in midtown. The hard-hats had swarmed out onto the street to break up the protest. The result had been a pitched battle that resulted in severe injuries to several of the battlers. Luther Downing served time in jail as the leader of the protest. An effort was made to charge him with attempted murder, but the District Attorney's office couldn't make a case against him stick. The hard-hats had never let up. They had picketed every public appearance Downing made. Now fifty or more of them had seen him shot to death on the sidewalk outside the Beaumont. The shots fired from a passing car by the killer had scarcely stopped echoing across Fifth Avenue to the Park than the hard-hats were gone, littering the street with their discarded signs and posters.

One of them remained. He was an infiltrator, placed there by the police, who had been fearful of just such an outcome to Downing's career. He was a dingy little man with a heavy brush mustache named Greenbaum. He had attempted to stand guard over the fallen

Downing and been pretty badly mauled by some of the crowd who had been watching the cameramen at work and had assumed that the hard-hats were responsible for the bloody killing. He and Waters, the doorman, were hustled into Doc Partridge's office off the lobby as soon as Hardy had control of things. Chambrun, concerned for Waters and the hotel, and I went with them and listened to Greenbaum's story while the doctor probed Waters' shoulder for a bullet.

"It was all too fast to give you a very clear picture, Lieutenant," Greenbaum told Hardy. He was holding an icebag to a badly bruised cheek. "There was nothing in particular going on. The hard-hats were just marching up and down outside the hotel, pretty bored. They were expecting to be relieved in about an hour by another group. I don't think they dreamed Downing would show his face outside the hotel."

"But he did, and he knew they were there," Hardy said.

"He didn't know about me," Greenbaum said, "but he knew there were four or five cops hanging around, and a patrol car that went by every few minutes. He must have thought he was safe enough."

"So he walks out the door and somebody lets him have it," Hardy said.

"All I can tell you is that none of the hard-hats expected him to show. None of the marchers was carrying a machine pistol. You can't hide one of those things in your hip pocket. It was my job to look for anything like that." Greenbaum winced as the icebag touched a particularly tender spot.

"The car?" Hardy said.

"That's where it gets tough," Greenbaum said. "It was either a crazy piece of luck for the killer, or—"

"Or he knew exactly when Downing was going to appear," Chambrun said in a flat, cold voice. "Had you seen a car cruising back and forth?"

"No," Greenbaum said. "I'd have noticed a car that kept appearing and reappearing. Thing is, I didn't actually see Downing come out the revolving door. I was talking to somebody, carrying my sign, when I heard the shots. I turned around and saw both Downing and the doorman down on the sidewalk. I heard tires screeching and I saw this black sedan taking off, with someone inside it firing a couple of last shots at Downing."

"License number?" Hardy asked.

"I'm sorry, Lieutenant. It was all so fast and I was being pushed and shoved. The guy next to me said, 'Jesus, someone got him! Let's get the hell out of here.' It was like a stampede, them all taking off in all directions."

"Kind of car?"

"A compact. Maybe a Chevrolet or a Dodge. Black. There were two people in it—the driver and the man with the machine pistol. I didn't get a clear look at either of them. It was all so fast."

"So you said."

"I'm sorry, Lieutenant. I had no reason to expect anything like that to happen. I tried to get to Downing. I forgot I still had on my hard-hat. All of a sudden half a dozen people were trying to beat the hell out of me."

"We better have a list of the people who were running the protest," Hardy said.

"Fellow they call Duke—Duke Dakin. He's kind of a shop steward for the union. We took orders from him, but he wasn't there when it happened."

"Maybe he was in the car," Hardy said.

"I couldn't get a good-enough look to tell you that, Lieutenant."

"I want him," Hardy said. "Have him picked up—when you get your face fixed."

Waters, the doorman, was in more trouble than Greenbaum. There was a bullet in his shoulder and Doc Partridge wanted him taken to the hospital.

"He needs a proper anesthetic before we start probing around for it," the doctor said. "Think you can make it all right in a taxi, Waters? I'll go with you, of course."

Waters nodded, his teeth gritted. The doctor went to the telephone to order a cab. Waters has been the day-time doorman on that Fifth Avenue side ever since I can remember. His job involves a good deal more than opening and closing the doors of cabs and automobiles. You might say he is the first greeter at the Beaumont. He presents you with your first taste of courtesy and good cheer. He is the first one to handle your luggage if you have any. He has to remember faces and the names that go with them. Ask him any day and he can tell you without a slip who has come and who has gone on his tour of duty.

"Did you see the car, Emmet?" Chambrun asked him.

I hadn't known Waters had a first name until then.

"A Dodge Dart, I think," Waters said. "I had just greeted the Fergusons and turned over their luggage to the bell captain. I remember Johnny had gone in the revolving door with the luggage when Downing came out. He and Johnny were both in the door at the same time, Johnny going in and Downing coming out. I remember I said to Downing, 'You're liable to get quite a reception out here, Mr. Downing.' He just smiled at me and said something about 'their bark—and their bite.' I asked him if he wanted a cab, and he said he did. I turned and beckoned to a cab in the line, but before the driver could move forward, this little black Dart swerved in and—all hell broke loose. I saw Downing was hit and I tried to move in to help him. That's when they got me."

"But you can't identify the gunman or the driver?"

"I'm sorry, Mr. Chambrun."

"Don't worry about it," Chambrun said. "You go to the hospital with Dr. Partridge and get yourself tended to. Private room if it's necessary to stay, Doc. And if you remember anything you think might be helpful, Emmet, let me know."

"Will do, Mr. Chambrun." Waters hesitated. "An opinion isn't what would interest you."

"Of course it would interest me."

"Well, sir, I don't think the hard-hats had anything to do with it."

"What makes you think not?" Chambrun asked.

"I know those guys," Waters said. "Grew up with their fathers. They're tough, loud, enjoy nothing more than a good free-for-all, specially if it's in the corner saloon. But set up a man and gun him down? It isn't their style, Mr. Chambrun.''

The doctor, who had put Waters' arm in a black silk sling, led his patient away. Miss Potter, the staff nurse, was applying some medication to Greenbaum's damaged cheek.

''I'm inclined to agree with Waters,'' Greenbaum said to Hardy. ''Those characters would have loved nothing better than to beat up on Downing. Dakin, their boss, had them worked up pretty good. But these aren't the Mafia, the underworld, the kind who hire hit-men. They got wives and kids and family responsibilities. Like Waters said, they love a brawl. But murder isn't their thing.''

''Could be. But I want Dakin here, and in a hurry. Tell Sergeant Fletcher where he can find him.'' Hardy drew a deep breath. ''Now let's hope when those TV cameramen process their films we come up with help—a face, a license number, a something.''

Chambrun's face had that carved stone look to it. His eyes were like slits cut in a mask. ''I'm not hopeful. The cameras had no reason to be focused on the car till it was taking off. I doubt a recognizable face, I doubt a license number that will do us any good. It will turn out to be a stolen car if there is a visible plate. No, I'm more interested in knowing where Downing was going, and who knew that he was going and exactly when.''

''You think he was suckered out and they were waiting for him, knowing just when he'd be coming?'' Hardy asked.

"What else?" Chambrun shrugged. "I damn well want to know what's going on up there on Fourteen."

Hardy's blond eyebrows rose. "You don't see any connection between this and the Watson kid, do you?"

"Marilyn saw something and got herself killed for that mishap," Chambrun said. "I suggest that Luther Downing saw something and got himself killed."

"You're playing games without any facts," Hardy said.

"I've learned one thing in a long life, Lieutenant. It may just be that there is no such thing in this world as a coincidence."

ONE NIGHT, long ago, I found myself up to my waist in swamp mud in an Indochinese jungle, knowing that I was surrounded in the blackness by Viet Cong snipers, listening, probably, for the sound of my breathing. No way out. I had a number of choices, none of them worth a damn. I remember lying there, soaked to the skin, terrified that a water snake might slither over my hand and that I wouldn't be able to keep from screaming. I'm not kidding when I say that I was almost more afraid of snakes than I was of the Viet Cong, who would probably de-ball me with their bayonets if they spotted me. Long afterwards I said I had discovered a new law which I chose to call the Haskell Dilemma. I could select any one of several ways to die, but nothing good. The Haskell Dilemma brought about another law. If you can't make a good choice, don't choose anything. Just let it happen. Maybe God will think of something.

How I got out of that swamp in one piece is another story for another time. That late afternoon, with an innocent little girl and perhaps not so innocent black poet in the Medical Examiner's autopsy rooms, I didn't want any more of whatever was going on. I wanted a bath, and a couple of stiff drinks, and delightful Carol Failes in my bed—or hers. Let Chambrun and Hardy kick around the Fourteen Dilemma. Giving it a name was about the only constructive thing I could think of doing.

But there were people scarred by tragedy: Helen Watson and possibly even George Watson. There must be someone who cared for Luther Downing. "I have friends," he had told Chambrun and me, as though we might think that unlikely because he was black—and angry. And there was my Carol, still up there on Fourteen with Helen Watson. She needed rescuing. With that in mind I got almost nowhere toward helping her right away.

As I stepped out of the dispensary, I found the Beaumont's lobby engulfed in a kind of hysteria. People who didn't belong there had come in off the street. They all wanted to get into the act, all claimed to have seen something of vital importance. They were swarming around Jerry Dodd and his staff, elbowing the indignant but somewhat disturbed guests who were trying to find out what had happened and what was being done about it. I didn't want anyone to flag me down and I lowered my head and sort of bullied my way toward the bank of elevators at the south side of the lobby. I saw one of the operators about to close his elevator's doors and I shouted to him to wait. He probably would have ignored anyone else, but I was part of the boss hierarchy. I moved quickly into the car and saw that there was another passenger. He was an older man about six feet tall, my height, slightly stooped and wearing tinted, wire-rimmed glasses. He gave me a blank look and then we both spoke to the operator at the same time. We both said, "Fourteen!"

The elevators move up with an almost inaudible swish, a trifle too quick if you have a tender stomach. I took a sidewise glance at my companion and realized it wasn't the rise of the elevator that troubled my gut. The man was Henry Bowers, or Kuglemann, or whatever, assassin and bomber, if Jasmine Gilhooly was to be believed.

The elevator stopped at Fourteen, and the doors slid noiselessly open. I turned to wait for Bowers to get off. He gave me a polite little gesture suggesting that I go first. I insisted, without words that he go first. Alphonse—Gaston. I don't remember now how it worked out. I know that we were suddenly standing together at the south end of the corridor. He smiled at me.

"Mr. Haskell? I think you'd better let Mr. Chambrun know that I'm back in the hotel," he said. He didn't tell me who he was. He knew I knew. He preceded me down the hall and let himself into his room. I headed for Suite E. I could have used the phone in the housekeeper's room but, for some reason, it didn't occur to me. I rang the E doorbell, and after a moment Carol opened the door to me. The way her face lit up would have made me very happy at some other time.

"Oh, God, Mark, am I glad to see you," she said.

"I've got to use your phone before I can talk," I said.

I could see that wasn't the reaction she expected.

"The living room," she said. "Dr. Partridge gave Helen something and she finally took it. She's asleep in one of the bedrooms."

"George Watson?" I asked on the move.

"No sign of him. He made his statement to the police somewhere else and he hasn't come back."

"You know about the shooting?" I asked. I was at the phone.

"What shooting?"

I asked to be put through to Chambrun, and seconds later I had him. "Bowers is back," I told him.

"Where?"

"He's in his room. He suggested I call you."

"Where are you?"

"Suite E on Fourteen."

"Meet me at Bowers' suite," Chambrun said. "I'm on my way."

I put down the phone and turned to Carol.

"What shooting?" she asked.

I put my arms around her and held her very close for a moment. Maybe I kissed her. I honestly don't remember. Maybe I just whispered something reassuring. Then I told her about Luther Downing, and I could feel her body start to tremble against mine.

"Oh, my God, Mark," she said.

"I'm going to send someone up here to stay with Mrs. Watson," I said. "You've had enough of this." I fished the key to my apartment out of my pocket. "You go down to my place and wait. No matter how long it takes me, wait."

"I think I'd rather go home," she said.

"No point. They'll only bring you back. You're on the list of people to be questioned. I've got to meet Chambrun out in the hall. Sit tight, love."

She didn't want to let me go. Her fingers were biting into my arms. "This is some kind of nightmare, Mark," she said.

"Nightmares always come to an end," I said, and didn't believe a word of it as I said it.

I WASN'T TOO REASSURED when, a few moments later, Chambrun got off the elevator and came down the hall toward me. He was alone. I'd have felt better if he'd had Hardy or Fletcher or Jerry Dodd with him. Bowers looked mild enough, but his reputation, via Jasmine Gilhooly, was anything but comforting. Then I remembered that the dapper little man coming toward me, a flower in the lapel of his dark blue tropical worsted suit, had spent an earlier part of his life stringing up Nazi soldiers on the Paris lampposts in the dead of night. Bowers would hold no terrors for Pierre Chambrun.

A raised eyebrow asked me whether Bowers was still where he was supposed to be.

I said he was, and that I would like to get someone to relieve Carol in the Watson suite. "She's had about all she can take of this," I said.

"Call Ruysdale—when there's an opportunity," Chambrun said, and rang Bowers' doorbell.

Bowers must have been standing on the other side of the door, because it was instantly opened and he faced us, staring at us mildly through his tinted glasses.

"Come in, gentlemen," he said, and opened the door wide.

We walked into Suite I.

"I'm afraid I can't offer you any hospitality," Bowers said. "I've been in touch with Sandberg and he warned me you'd be wanting to ask me questions. It seems the lady next door claims to have identified me out of her past."

Now Chambrun hadn't told Sandberg, the State Department man, who had told us about Bowers. He had refused on grounds that it might place his informant in danger. Bowers gave us a patient smile.

"Who else but Mrs. Gilhooly?" he asked. "Won't you sit down gentlemen."

I asked if I could use his phone and he waved at the instrument on the corner table. "Unless you need privacy," he said. "In which case there are the bedroom phones."

Chambrun didn't look pleased by the interruption. "Call from here," he said.

I asked the switchboard to connect me with Miss Ruysdale. Chambrun and Bowers seemed to be assessing each other, like two fighters in their corners of the ring, waiting for the bell. I told Betsy Ruysdale what I wanted and hung up the receiver.

"You know what's happened to Downing?" Chambrun asked in a flat, cold voice.

Bowers nodded. "I came through the lobby just now," he said. "A fairly clean job, by all accounts."

I remember I was studying him, looking for a bulge under his jacket that would tell me he was carrying a gun. He wasn't, or that sloppy-looking summer tweed was expertly tailored to hide it.

"You are going to ask me why I am here in your hotel, Mr. Chambrun," Bowers said, "and, regretfully, I'm going to have to refuse to tell you."

"With two murders on our hands, coupled with your reputation, I'm afraid the police are going to insist."

Bowers shrugged. He was so relaxed it was almost frightening. "If they want answers about me, Mr. Chambrun, they'll have to get them from my principal, Mr. Sandberg. It shouldn't be too long from now. He's already on the shuttle flight from Washington."

Chambrun took the silver case from his pocket and lit one of his flat Egyptian cigarettes. I expected him to boil over. He didn't.

"At the very least you're here to watch someone," he said. "Is your job over now?"

"If you mean will I be removed because my cover is broken," Bowers said, "that's another answer that will have to come from my principal. Quite frankly, I don't know the answer to that yet." He smiled faintly. "If you're asking if my job is over because Luther Downing is dead, you surely couldn't expect me to admit to that."

"Nor to the murder of the unlucky Watson child," Chambrun said.

"Nor to that," Bowers said, his smile widening.

"But your principal, as you call Sandberg, requested that you be placed in a suite on this floor, not any suite in the hotel. So someone on this floor is your reason for being here."

"A logical assumption," Bowers said.

"We are strangling on the lack of the oxygen of facts," Chambrun said. "You can help us, Mr. Bowers, if you will, without betraying yourself or your principal."

Bowers looked interested. "How?" he asked.

"The way you people work is no mystery to me," Chambrun said. "You are here to watch someone, to cover someone's activities. You register under a false name—a John Smith. It's obvious the man you're watching doesn't know you by sight. But once established here you would want to know all you could about the other people on the floor; whether any of them were a threat of any sort to you and your job. You've researched every one of them."

"And made a bad judgment," Bowers said. "I didn't think, after twenty years, that Mrs. Gilhooly would recognize me. Age has changed me, and I make a professional effort to constantly alter my appearance. But—the lady spotted me the first time we came face to face."

"You must have had a sexual electricity for Jasmine," Chambrun said.

I couldn't believe the way he was handling Bowers, almost like an old friend.

"It was a close thing—long ago," Bowers said. He chuckled. "Perhaps not as close as your experience."

"I was very young," Chambrun said. "I wanted the job of running this hotel more than anything, including Cleopatra had she been available." He smiled his number-one bland smile. "But I see I have been a subject of your research."

Bowers nodded. "In my business, if you're not in your own ball park, you can't allow yourself to be at the mercy of the whims of your host—to mix a metaphor. So, yes, I did some checking on you, Chambrun, before I ever registered here."

"And your business is terror, murder, bombings," Chambrun said in the same casual voice, but I saw that his eyes had turned cold as two newly minted dimes. "I suppose there are dossiers on me in all kinds of places like the CIA, the FBI, to which you have access, thanks to the help of your principal."

Bowers' smile was gone. He recognized that the gloves were off. "There are sources on most people of any consequence. You have a reputation as an expert in terror yourself, Chambrun—thirty-odd years ago in Paris. The French Resistance."

"Which is why I understand you," Chambrun said. "Why I know just exactly how you will behave in this situation. There is a file on you, too, Count von Zedwitz. That was your name in those days, wasn't it? There are men in France today who have still not given up the dream of punishing the Nazi war criminals who raped their women, burned their homes, shot their sons in cold blood. One word on the long distance phone to Paris and you will be very lucky to stay alive for another twenty-four hours.''

Right between the eyes, I thought. Chambrun must already have been on the long distance phone. Kugle-mann and an airport in Romania had been enough of a lead for one of his old companions in France to give Bowers his proper name and, probably, a further list of his crimes, Chambrun, the magician, never failed to produce a rabbit out of his hat.

I have to hand it to Bowers. He took it without blinking. ''You seem to have done your homework too,'' he said. I thought a subtle change had come over him. He had seemed so relaxed and now there was a kind of wiry tension about him. I have seen it in ath-letes, so loose between plays they look as if they might collapse, and then, as the next play begins, ready to explode.

''I never try to make a trade,'' Chambrun said, ''without having something to offer.''

''The only thing you could offer me is silence,'' Bowers said. ''Why would you?''

''Because I want something from you,'' Chambrun said, ''and because I disagree with my friends that we should still be fighting World War Two. You, with your special gifts, might kill some of them before they get you. I could be persuaded to save them even if it meant saving you.''

''What exactly do you want from me?'' Bowers asked. He was a man weighing his options.

''What's going on on this floor, to start with,'' Chambrun said. ''What did that twelve-year-old child see that made it necessary to kill her? Why was

Downing hit? I choose not to believe that the two things are unrelated. It would take me a week, maybe more, to do an in-depth on all the people on this floor. You've already done it. I want your results now, before I leave this room.''

Bowers stared at his opponent for a minute. "You will check out on what I tell you," he said. "I will have to be evasive about someone or give away my reason for being here. You will find me out sooner or later."

"Whatever is going on here has to be stopped," Chambrun said. "If your business is connected to these killings, God help you anyway. If it isn't connected, it's none of my business."

"And how can I trust you?" Bowers asked.

Chambrun made an impatient gesture and snuffed out his cigarette in an ash tray on the coffee table. "If you've really researched me, you'll know that if I make a deal I'll go through with it. If you don't know that, you've done a lousy job, and maybe nothing you will tell me is worth hearing. I think you're much too good at your job to have asked me a foolish question."

"In my job nobody ever tells anyone the truth," Bowers said. "However—let's take the most easily disposed of first. The Watsons. Small town in the West, may never have been more than a hundred miles away from it till they won their lottery; Watson a big frog in a very small pond, without what it takes to make good in a real world. In a rage, Watson might kill his wife or his child; he might even kill Downing if he believed Downing, a black man, had been molesting his child. But he isn't up to a skillfully planned assassination. I buy your theory. The child saw some-thing."

"What?"

"I don't know that—yet," Bowers said. "Let's move on to Jasmine Gilhooly." A smile twitched the corners of his mouth. "She couldn't kill a child if the child saw her stealing the crown jewels. She couldn't kill, period. The Watsons and Mrs. Gilhooly are surely innocent bystanders."

"Would you kill Jasmine to keep her silent?" Chambrun asked.

"It's too late," Bowers said quietly. "I don't kill for revenge—like your friends in Paris." He frowned. "Perhaps we should take Luther Downing next, be-cause surely he didn't kill anyone."

"You don't think the hard-hats—?"

"No," Bowers said. "They might beat him up, tar and feathers if they're still in fashion, but a slick, professional assassination, never. But it's entirely possible his murder has nothing to do with what's going on in your hotel, Chambrun. He has a colorful history that caused me some alarm when I found I had him as a neighbor on this floor. It was entirely possi-ble his presence here might be connected with what brought me here."

"Which was—?"

"Sorry," Bowers said. "That isn't part of our deal. But Downing is—was—interesting. He was a genuine revolutionary who hated the Establishment for what has been done to blacks in this country for two hundred years. He was passionately opposed to war, particularly the war in Vietnam. He thought the Es-

tablishment was perfectly willing to slaughter
hundreds of thousands of Vietnamese for whatever
reason because they were not white Anglo-Saxon
Protestants. He staged riots at political conventions.
He went to jail fifty times for his activities, got out,
started all over again. He was honest in his convictions but he was a man of violence, just as violent as
the people he hated. He didn't limit his battle to Watts,
or Bedford Stuyvesant, or Harlem. He fought the Establishment in the Congo, in Algiers, in South Af-
rica. He was an international figure. Recently he has
had one passion, one target: Henry Kissinger, whom
he thought of as a modern Bismarck. It's not a secret
that his tirades against Kissinger have resulted in
constant surveillance for the last months. He came
here to read poetry to his revolutionary followers, but
I suspect he chose the Beaumont because key figures
in the United Nations circulate here, both his friends
and his enemies. It wouldn't be absurd that some kind
of explosion was being planned here, Chambrun.
Word got out to Downing's enemies and they set him
up.''

"And his enemies could be the CIA, the FBI.''

"Could be.''

"Or the State Department,'' Chambrun said, his
voice edged.

Bowers smiled at him. "Could be,'' he said, "but
Downing wasn't my assignment.''

"You've promised you'll lie about someone,''
Chambrun said. "But, since you've brought up international connections, what about the two on this
floor? Begin with Nikos Parrasis.''

Bowers nodded slowly. "He is richer than some governments," he said. "Maybe I should say most governments, because he owes no one, has no budget deficits. Scheming for power and money is mother's milk to him. A thousand people would like to cut out his heart, if he has one, which is why he doesn't even go to the bathroom without his personal bodyguard. I don't know what he is up to now, but automatically you know he is up to something, and that if you get in his way, George Panzer, the guard, will throw you off the roof or dispose of you in some equally flamboyant fashion. Parrasis doesn't wait to make sure you're interested in him. If he just suspects it, you've had it."

"Panzer?"

"A completely cold-blooded killer," Bowers said. "He is so quick on the trigger you are lucky he didn't kill one of your maids who let herself into the suite to give them clean towels, thinking they were out. Panzer doesn't worry about mistakes. Better to kill someone by mistake than to have something happen to his beloved employer. But if you are trying to connect George Panzer, the lunatic bodyguard, with Downing's death, I say no. I picked up some gossip in the lobby. There were two people in that murder car, I hear—the driver and the gunman. That puts aside Panzer for me; he would never have an accomplice. He does what he does alone."

"If Parrasis wanted Downing out of the way, he'd have no trouble hiring a hit-man," Chambrun said.

"He can afford any man's price for anything he wants done," Bowers said.

"And so we come to Abdel Ghorra," Chambrun said.

"Ghorra is oil," Bowers said, "and oil is the name of today's international game. It is a weapon, an instrument for blackmail. It has raised men of no consequence to be princes of the world. The great multinational corporations forget about patriotism, forget about morals, when they smell oil. Ghorra is, you might say, a traveling salesman in a burnoose. He has only to lift his finger to get anything he wants in today's world, from a thousand percent profit on his product to treachery from men in high places. He can destroy your country's economy by crossing out the numbers on your filling station's gas pumps and writing in bigger ones. It's not just Ghorra, you understand, but the people he represents. Get rid of him and a new man, wearing a different burnoose, will take his place."

"The State Department would be interested in him," Chambrun said.

Bowers smiled. "Could be—undoubtedly is. Wouldn't be doing their job if they weren't."

Chambrun returned the smile. "I won't ask," he said. "The bridge players?"

"The most innocent-looking and the most complex guests on your fourteenth floor, Chambrun. They have names, but they are referred to as the American Team. Winston, Stein, Lessigore, and MacMartin; those are the names, but I'm not sure what name goes with what face. They are all of a type. They could be four intense scientists or mathematicians. They have computers for brains. They know the odds on any fall of the cards, and probably the odds on anything else in the world happening a certain way. What they say doesn't mean what it seems to say. 'I bid a club,' doesn't mean I have clubs. It means I have hearts and spades and want my partner to take his pick. Intentions concealed by conventions.''

''Except that everyone knows what the conventions mean,'' Chambrun said.

''At the game of bridge,'' Bowers conceded. ''They play it here, and in Rome, and in London, and in Israel. 'We are the American Team.' But is that a convention that disguises a truth? They must play the game of bridge well enough to keep circulating around the world, ostensibly representing the United States. I suggest they may be couriers for a criminal conspiracy; arms, drugs, take your pick. They sit at green baize tables, studying their cards, playing them skillfully, and listening for something far more important, their orders from the top. Customs have searched their luggage for heroin, for diamonds, for contraband of any kind. No luck. But wherever they have just left, something seems to happen very shortly afterwards. They have carried the word, given the signal. Something has happened here.''

''I should think the State Department would lift their passports if this is all so obvious?''

''The State Department, the FBI, Interpol, the police of all countries suffer from a common disease,'' Bowers said. ''They want the big fish, the head men, the kings and queens of crime. They are convinced that sooner or later the little fish will lead them to the people they want, so they let them keep swimming.

That's why the little fish do so very well. They are allowed to function and they almost never lead anyone to anyone at the top of the heap. If they were not clever, the big fish would swallow them up. The American Team are far more devious than their bridge conventions, Chambrun.''

Chambrun reached for his silver case again. ''That leaves us with the French lady and her troop.''

Bowers actually laughed. ''Yvonne Darcel! My God, Chambrun, did you ever see any of her early films?''

''No.''

''Simple, unpretentious pornography. Sex in endlessly impossible positions, accompanied by a pseudo-scientific lecture on sex as a family institution. She was right out of some sort of brothel in Marseilles, maybe eighteen years old. The place was run by Paul Martine, who now calls himself her husband. He got her a chance in those porno films. Some arty film director saw her. He had a film coming up that called for a nude scene. He was interested in a body, not an actress. Yvonne has an unbelievably beautiful body. It turned out, given a small chance by the director, that she had some real talent as an actress. And so—to the top. Because she is what she is, she plays all the traditional temperamental games of a star. What she really is is that rare delight, a whore who enjoys her work. She acts well, she cavorts in public, and she sleeps with a different man every night. It is up to Martine to supply her.''

Chambrun took a drag on his cigarette. ''You say Paul Martine 'calls himself' Yvonne's husband?''

"It's a technicality," Bowers said. "Whether or not they ever took the vows I can't tell you, but Martine is, purely and simply, her business manager without any marital privileges."

"I had the Englishman, Chip Nelson, written down as her lover," Chambrun said.

"May have been," Bowers said with a shrug, "but long ago passed over. Nelson was a professional athlete, race car driver, soccer player. Yvonne goes for the athletic type. Now Nelson is a combination bodyguard, baggage handler, and go-for—go for a cup of coffee, go for the latest boy friend. Yvonne doesn't have to arrange her own love life. Martine and Nelson pimp for her."

"The secretary, the girl who doubles, Marie Orell?"

"Nature plays strange tricks on people," Bowers said. "Marie Orell wants to be an actress, and from what I've heard, she is a very good one. But Nature played a dirty trick on her. She looks so much like Yvonne that no film producer in Europe or here in the United States would touch her. It's possible that if Marie had made it first it would be Yvonne who couldn't get work—except, of course, with her basic talents as a prostitute. Marie had no choice except to go to work for Yvonne. She hates Yvonne. She can't even have the sweet revenge of stealing a lover from Yvonne. One-night stands are Yvonne's specialty. After one night she throws away men like empty beer cans."

"I had the idea that Marie and Chip Nelson were on pretty intimate terms," Chambrun said. He had evidently noticed the thigh-stroking too.

"It's at least a convenient arrangement," Bowers said. He sighed. "I wonder if I have helped you at all? Because that's the bottom line on what I know."

"Except, of course, one of your little thumbnail sketches is a lie," Chambrun said.

Bowers gave us a tired smile. "The first thing you will do, Chambrun, is double-check what I've told you. So it wouldn't be very clever of me to tell you an obvious lie. I can't know everything there is to know about any one of these people. So each of these what you call 'sketches' is incomplete. In one instance I have withheld facts, but nothing I have told you is a lie."

"Considering that you have been practicing your particular trade for a great many years without being wiped out marks you as a very clever man, Mr. Bowers. But I promise you, if what you have left out of your recital is knowledge of what Marilyn Watson saw that made it necessary to kill her, or why Luther Downing was hit, then I will consider you an accessory to murder, and you will have slipped away for the last time."

"Let me assure you, Chambrun, I know nothing about nor am I in any way connected with the two killings."

Chambrun gave him a cold smile. "You would assure me you were the mother of twins if it would suit your purposes," he said.

TWO

Miss Ruysdale was in her reception room office when we got back there. Chambrun had been lost in his own thoughts on the way down from Fourteen, not speaking a word to me.

"Lieutenant Hardy is in your office," Miss Ruysdale told him. "He's questioning the hard-hat foreman."

Chambrun's face clouded. "I thought we'd provided him with an office on the main floor."

"It's pretty much of a madhouse down there," Miss Ruysdale said. "People in and out. It occurred to me that it might please you to know exactly how he's proceeding."

So help me, he was fighting a smile. "You are almost as devious as the man we just left, Ruysdale," he said.

She gave him her Mona Lisa smile which suggested a whole private world between them that none of the rest of us at the Beaumont knew about.

"Your gal has been relieved, Mark," she said to me.

I thanked her and followed Chambrun into his office. Hardy was leaning against the carved Florentine desk, his attention focused on a powerfully built red-faced man who sat in one of the green leather armchairs. The detective glanced at Chambrun.

"You mind my being in here?" he asked.

"Not if you don't mind our joining you," Chambrun said.

"Be my guest," Hardy said dryly. "This is Duke Dakin. He was in charge of that protest gathering outside the hotel."

Dakin glared at Chambrun. "We didn't make no trouble out there," he said. He looked like my concept of the old-fashioned village blacksmith. He could bend iron bars.

"I've explained to Dakin that, as of now, we don't believe his people had anything to do with the hit on Downing," Hardy said. "But there were fifty or sixty men out there, carrying signs. They can't all have been looking in the same direction at once. That car with the killer in it was waiting for Downing, somewhere near the hotel. Not cruising back and forth, as we know from Greenbaum."

"That sonofabitch," Dakin growled. "All the time he was a cop!"

"And is convinced we don't have to concentrate on you," Hardy said. "You're lucky he was there. What I'm getting at, Dakin, is that one of those sixty men has to have noticed the car, wondered about it, might even be able to identify the people in it. When you're hanging around someplace for hours, you notice little things. I need your help. I want you to get together the men who were there this afternoon and put it on the line to them. An innocent child was murdered here this morning, and then Downing. We think the crimes were connected. See what you can find out for us."

"My guys aren't going to be too willing to help the cops," Dakin said.

Chambrun was at the sideboard, pouring himself a cup of that foul Turkish coffee. He turned toward Dakin. "We may be satisfied that you and your people had nothing to do with the killing, Dakin," he said, "but until we find the killer, half the people in the United States are going to believe you did. I suggest you try to get some of the mud off your clothes."

"I could pull in your whole goddamned union and throw them in a tank downtown," Hardy said. "It would take a month to question them all. You've got a choice, Dakin."

Dakin made up his mind then and there. "It'll take a couple of hours or maybe more to get them together. Some of 'em are likely out on the town, boozing it up. I'll do what I can. Get in touch if anyone saw something."

"Time is what we haven't got any of," Hardy said. "Move it, friend."

Dakin took off.

Chambrun came over to his desk, balancing his coffee cup in the palm of his hand. "Anything from the photographers who were outside the hotel?" he asked.

"Soon," Hardy said. "I'm not hopeful of the results. The rear of the car and the back of a couple of heads."

"And now perhaps you'll tell me why you didn't join me in Bowers' suite," Chambrun said. "I sent Jerry to tell you."

Hardy looked down at the knuckles of his big hands. "Orders," he said.

"What orders?"

"From the top. I am to leave Bowers alone until your friend Sandberg gets here from Washington."

Chambrun's coffee cup rattled as he put it down hard on his desk. "I'm tempted to kick everyone on that floor out of the hotel," he said. "The longer they're all there together, the more chance there is of something else happening."

"Not yet," Hardy said. "You scatter them and I'm out of business. I couldn't hold one of them for five minutes if I arrested them."

Chambrun, with the irritation that comes from frustration, sat down at his desk and began to give Hardy a shortened version of the rundown Bowers had done on the people on Fourteen. I suddenly realized that it was dinnertime, and I was hungry, and I wanted a drink, and Carol was waiting for me in my apartment down the hall. I was wondering what could be done about my needs when Miss Ruysdale stuck her head in the door. She beckoned to me.

"Can you be spared?" she asked, when I joined her.

I allowed as how I could.

"Friend of yours in my office with something interesting," she said.

The friend was Mike Traynor, the *Newsview* man with whom I'd been having a drink in the Trapeze when Downing was shot. I thought he'd been luckier than I had. He'd clearly had a couple of drinks since then. He had a brown Manila envelope in his hands and out of it he took a copy of *Newsview*.

"I thought this might interest you, Mark—and the powers-that-be," he said.

He handed me the magazine. It was a back issue. It had a picture of Catfish Hunter, the Yankee pitcher, on the cover. I saw that it had a March date, training camp time for the ball clubs in Florida. The Catfish was being built up as a new New York idol in a feature story.

"Toward the middle, page fifty-six," Mike said.

I turned the pages and came on a half-page picture of Abdel Ghorra, his melancholy eyes staring at me out of his burnoose. The article was written by Peter Styles, *Newsview*'s top feature man, and was a study in depth of the whole Mid-East oil situation.

"You can read the piece when you have time," Mike said. "But there's a picture on the next page that should interest you."

I turned to look. There was a picture of a man standing in front of a large crowd on some sort of platform, obviously involved in delivering an impassioned speech. He was a dark, handsome guy who looked like a movie star. I glanced at the caption.

VICTOR MAGINOT INFLAMES A CROWD OF FRENCH LEFTISTS.

"When I got a list of the people on the fourteenth floor I remembered this piece in the magazine months ago," Mike said, "and I had it sent over from the office. When you read it, you'll find out all there is to know about Ghorra. Victor Maginot is a radical terrorist who's wanted in half a dozen countries. His particular target at that time was the Arab oil man. That you can also read about. I don't think you've looked closely at the picture, Mark. Sitting on the platform behind Maginot—"

I looked closer, and I saw what he was talking about. Behind Maginot, watching him intently, was Luther Downing.

"So it occurred to me there might be a connection between Ghorra and Downing," Mike said. "In that speech Maginot was urging a campaign of terror against the oil sheiks who were pricing the little men out of the energy they need to go to work, to live their lives, to light their homes and cook their meals. It's the kind of cause Downing would have backed. It's a pipe dream, Mark, but Downing could have been here to get Ghorra and, instead, Ghorra got him."

"Come with me," I said, and I took Mike back into the office where Chambrun and Hardy were still hassling.

I didn't read the article until much later, but the essence of it, cleverly put together by the writer, was a picture of the struggle between the Arab nations, in control of their own resources after centuries, and the rest of the industrialized world, its economy threatened by a kind of blackmail. An offshoot of this was the plight of the little man, brought up to depend on his automobile, his electricity, a dozen other things, suddenly unable, economically, to buy what he needs. The article had used personalities to symbolize each one of these forces. There was Abdel Ghorra, spokesman and horse trader for oil; there was the head of Quadrant International, one of the huge multinational corporations, trying to bypass governments for the sake of profits in dealing for oil; and there was Victor Maginot, the voice of the helpless little man, advocating a worldwide campaign of terror against the powerful and the greedy.

In the office I put down the copy of *Newsview* in front of Chambrun. Both he and Hardy knew Mike Traynor, so there was no time wasted in introductions. I pointed to the picture of Luther Downing sitting on the platform with Victor Maginot.

"One thing is certain," Chambrun said after a moment of scowling at the picture. "Downing knew who Ghorra is and why he's here. Ghorra was on Downing's enemies list."

"But it was Downing who was killed," Hardy said.

"Of course Ghorra would know who Downing was and would certainly consider him a threat," Mike Traynor said. "A friend and ally of Maginot's."

"And could buy his own assassins from any place in the world," Chambrun said.

Hardy looked at Chambrun. "Maginot is French," he said. "You know anything about him, Pierre?"

Chambrun's eyes were shadowed as he looked somewhere into the past. "I knew his father," he said. "He was a very tough freedom fighter back in the dark days." Chambrun always referred to the time of the Resistance in France as "the dark days." "The son I never met. He was an infant when I knew his father—who, incidentally, was shot to death on the streets of Marseilles just two days before the Germans surrendered."

"Maginot could only be involved in this indirectly," Mike Traynor said. "If you saw the afternoon paper, you'll know that he made a speech on the underground radio from Algiers about two o'clock today. It was the usual tirade against the Arab oil men in general, the big conglomerates, and—'' Mike stopped in the middle of a sentence. He smacked his forehead with the palm of his hand. ''God damn, but it went right by me when I glanced at the news ticker. He had a few unkind words to say about our Greek friend, Nikos Parrasis.''

''It's a small world,'' Hardy said after a moment.

I REMEMBER THINKING that I was starving, that Carol was waiting for me in my apartment down the hall, and that we seemed to have drifted a long way from a little girl who looked like Alice in Wonderland and who had been beaten to death. Maybe I'm a pretty ordinary kind of guy. I can be properly outraged over power struggles, and corporate greed, and political tricks and games, but I don't really understand them. Luther Downing, a revolutionary, had run whatever risks he ran knowingly. He got killed for taking them. That's an interesting historical fact, but I didn't feel very deeply about it. Marilyn Watson, a lovely, eager child, was something else again. Thinking about her was painful and started up a kind of smoldering anger.

I wanted to suggest to Chambrun that we get back to first things. To hell with Victor Maginot making speeches in Algiers; to hell with Abdel Ghorra here to make oil deals with someone; to hell with Nikos Parrasis and his mustachioed bodyguard. Let them have at each other. Let's get back to Marilyn and find the sonofabitch who'd crushed in her skull.

I didn't get to it because Jerry Dodd, accompanied by Mrs. Kniffin, the housekeeper on Fourteen, barged into the office.

"Maybe nothing," Jerry said to Chambrun, "but you ought to hear it." He gestured at Mrs. Kniffin.

Mrs. Kniffin had been through a rough day for a woman of her age and temperament. The fourteenth floor was her world, and it had been turned upside-down.

"What is it, Mrs. Kniffin?" Chambrun asked quite gently.

Mrs. Kniffin's mouth quivered out of control.

Jerry Dodd took the ball for her. "This afternoon, about four o'clock, Grace saw Luther Downing come out of Suite A—Yvonne Darcel's."

"That was long after the little girl was found," Mrs. Kniffin said. "I—I didn't think much about it. The French lady seems to know everybody. They belong in the same world, I guess; him a poet and she an actress. It seemed natural enough. But after I heard that Mr. Downing had been shot, I—I thought I better mention it to Mr. Dodd."

"Quite right," Chambrun said. "Can you be more precise about the time, Grace?"

"It was a little after four o'clock," Mrs. Kniffin said. "I didn't have any special reason to notice the time, Mr. Chambrun, but I do know the room service had just delivered an order to the Arab gentleman in H. They do have a delivery time marked on their slips."

"The door was open as usual—the lady noisy?"

"No, sir. He opened the door to come out and closed it behind him."

"Did you see Mr. Downing go into Miss Darcel's suite?"

"No, sir."

"So you don't know how long he'd been in there when you saw him come out?"

"No, sir."

Chambrun glanced at Hardy. "Didn't you have the floor covered, Lieutenant?"

Hardy was frowning at his notebook. "By four o'clock everyone had provided us with written statements," he said. "People were free to come and go. I had a man stationed by the elevators who can tell us who had left the floor, but he had no reason to be watching the corridor."

"Can he tell us who's up there now?"

Hardy nodded and went over to the phone.

"You'd better go home, Grace, and get some rest," Chambrun said to Mrs. Kniffin. "We'll have someone take over for you."

"It'll be time to turn down the beds soon and check the linen," Mrs. Kniffin said.

"The maids can handle it this once without your supervision," Chambrun said. "Go home, Grace. That's an order."

She took off, fighting tears.

Hardy was getting information from his man on the phone, and presently he hung up. "Miss Orell is in the Darcel suites, along with the maids," he said. "Darcel and the two men took off somewhere. They mentioned a film showing, didn't they? Mrs. Watson is in her suite, along with Miss Simmons, who took Carol Failes' place. Ghorra is in H. Bowers is next door. Mrs. Gilhooly went down to the lobby about five minutes ago. The rest are absent and unaccounted for."

"I think perhaps we'd better have a chat with Miss Orell," Chambrun said.

One of those farcical French maids opened the door to Suite A when Chambrun, Hardy and I got there. She blinked her long lashes at us and told us Miss Darcel "ees go out." Chambrun spoke to her in French, sharply, with the information that we wanted Mlle. Orell, and the maid's high heels tip-tapped down the hall in a hurry. Then Marie Orell appeared. She had changed out of the pink linen suit into a becoming black dinner dress, cut low enough in front to reveal the fact that her measurements were just as spectacular as Yvonne Darcel's. The look-alike thing was a shade confusing.

"You have been told that Yvonne is not in," she said to Chambrun.

"I think you can tell us what we want to know, Miss Orell," Chambrun said, and walked into the living room without waiting for an invitation. Hardy and I followed him. I imagine Chambrun considered that this was his room, not hers. I think he thought of all the rooms in the hotel as his.

"What is it you want?" Marie asked. Her English was better than Yvonne's, her voice cool and unruffled. She didn't use her hands as a part of her conversational equipment. They hung, relaxed, at her sides.

"We have just learned that Luther Downing was a visitor to this suite a little after four this afternoon," Chambrun said.

"Who is Luther Downing?" she asked.

"That was just about an hour before he was shot dead outside the hotel," Chambrun said.

"Ah, the black man," she said. "A terrible affair."

"Was he a friend of Yvonne's?" Chambrun asked.

"Friend?" Marie's eyebrows shot upward. "The black man?"

"He was seen coming out of here, Miss Orell. It isn't a far-out question," Hardy said. "Was Downing a friend of Miss Darcel's, or perhaps yours, or someone else's in the suite? Mr. Martine's or Mr. Nelson's? The maids'?"

"Of course not," the girl said, and if she wasn't angry, she was giving a good imitation. "Your question surprised me, Mr. Chambrun. Friend! But yes, the black man was in here this afternoon, and Yvonne was beside herself with—with outrage!"

"Why?" Chambrun asked, dead-pan.

"He just wandered in!" Marie said. "He just walked into someone else's rooms without a by-your-leave."

"You leave the doors open," Chambrun said.

"But that isn't an invitation to strangers!"

"The child could have 'just wandered in,' too," Chambrun said. "But let that pass. Tell me about Downing. He 'just wandered in,' you say?"

"Yvonne walked into this room from her bedroom and there he was!" Marie said. "She could have been naked!"

"With the front door open?" Hardy asked gently.

"What did he want?" Chambrun asked.

"Who knows? An autograph, I suppose. Yvonne screamed at him, drove him out. The impertinence of his just coming in!"

"You were there? You saw it?" Chambrun asked.

"No. I was in my bedroom—in Suite B."

"So Yvonne told you what had happened, you didn't see it?"

"That is so."

"Because Yvonne didn't drive him out," Chambrun said. "He let himself out, closed the door behind him. We have a witness to that."

Marie shrugged her lovely shoulders. "If you say so, monsieur. I was not present. As I say, Yvonne told me about it afterwards."

"And she told you he wanted her autograph?"

"She assumed it, I think. She didn't give him a chance to say what he wanted, she told me."

Chambrun gave her a kind of baleful look, turned on his heel, and walked out of the room and into the corridor. It wasn't like him to ignore the simple courtesy of a "thank you."

"Please let me know when Miss Darcel gets back," Hardy said, and followed Chambrun out.

I gave Marie Orell what must have been a sort of sickly smile. "Lovely dress," I said. "It does wonders for you."

Out in the hall Chambrun was fuming. "Not a single word of truth in it," he said. "Downing was no autograph hunter. He didn't just 'wander in,' even if the door was open. And when he got in, the door was closed. It was closed sometime while he was in there, because Mrs. Kniffin saw him open it when he came out. He didn't go in there just to gawk at a sex queen. Why lie about it?"

"Bad publicity," I suggested. "They don't want Yvonne's name connected with a killing."

"I will connect it if they don't tell us the truth," Chambrun said. He tapped a cigarette on the back of his hand. "While we're here, let's have a go at the oil king."

HAVE YOU NOTICED, in pictures of Arab gentlemen who are suddenly very much in our consciousness, that they all seem to have warm, brown, almost gentle eyes? What my mother used to call "bedroom eyes"? Their mouths are sensuous, red-lipped, mobile, with a suggestion of hidden cruelty. We've had quite a few of them in the hotel and I've found them to be impeccably courteous, most of them British-educated, smooth, bland, revealing absolutely nothing about themselves.

Abdel Ghorra, who opened the door of Suite H to us, was all those things.

"Ah, Mr. Chambrun," he said. "And the police lieutenant. And I believe you are Mr. Haskell, the public relations man for the hotel?" He looked at me as if meeting me was an indescribable pleasure. "Do come in, gentlemen."

The first thing I was aware of as we went into the suite was that our Mr. Ghorra had been burning some kind of incense in the rooms. I had to admit it was preferable to the carbon monoxide fumes that constitute a major portion of New York's so-called fresh air.

There was a stretcher table in the center of the living room, and it was loaded down with papers and documents that looked like contracts, or leases, or mortgages, or God knows what. A crooked-neck desk light was focused on Ghorra's working space, even though there was still daylight at the windows.

"It is a disaster," Ghorra said in very British English, "to have to stay indoors working on such a lovely summer day." He gestured at the papers and documents.

"It has not been a lovely summer day for us," Chambrun said. This was Chambrun the hanging judge.

"Can I offer you refreshment of some sort?" Ghorra asked. "A drink, perhaps? It is that time of day."

"It is the time of day for some straight answers from you, Mr. Ghorra."

I couldn't decide whether those limpid eyes and the slightly twisted smile appearing from the burnoose that covered his head, his cheeks, and his shoulders, made him look like the villain in a Clint Eastwood movie or my grandmother's washerwoman.

"Answers to what, Mr. Chambrun?" he asked. "I have already told the Lieutenant all I know about the unfortunate little girl across the hall, which was precisely nothing."

"Were you aware that Luther Downing had a suite, also across the hall from you?"

"And who may Luther Downing be, Mr. Chambrun?" Ghorra asked, ever so polite.

Chambrun surprised me by pulling that old copy of *Newsview* out of an inside pocket and slapping it down on the stretcher table under Ghorra's nose. He pointed to the picture of Downing, sitting behind Maginot on some faraway platform.

"About an hour ago that man was shot to death outside the Fifth Avenue entrance of this hotel, Mr. Ghorra. I suggest you knew who he was. You knew he was a friend of a man who no later than early afternoon was delivering a tirade about you on the Algiers radio. I suggest you knew who Downing was, would have been suspicious of his presence here, would have kept a sharp watch on him, and just might have arranged to have him removed from the scene."

Those limpid brown eyes were suddenly narrow, glittering slits, and I forgot about my grandmother's washerwoman.

"I find your suggestions repellent to me, Mr. Chambrun." The voice was still smooth, but icy. "I have tried to cooperate with the Lieutenant about the little girl, but I should remind you both that I am here on a diplomatic passport and I am not required to answer any questions from you or anyone else."

"Diplomatic passports don't impress me, Mr. Ghorra, when blood is spilled in my house. Your refusal to talk reasonably about an explosive situation will be a part of the record. If there is further violence—"

"I must stand on my rights," Ghorra said.

"Are you aware that in the next suite to yours, Mr. Ghorra, is a man with a thirty-year record of assassinations, bombings, and cold-blooded murders?"

"It would surprise me a great deal if it is true," Ghorra said. "I would not have expected you to play host to that kind of guest."

"Like you, he has diplomatic protection," Chambrun said.

"Ah!"

"You refuse to tell me of any connection you may have with that man or any of the other guests on this floor?"

Ghorra spread his hands in a gesture of regret. "I have no connections with anyone on this floor. Until the excitement about the little girl, I had no idea who had the other rooms on Fourteen. In the milling around at the time I recognized Mr. Parrasis. I do not know him, you understand, but I have seen him more than once in various parts of the world. He is famous, no? I recognized the four gentlemen who represent your country at the bridge table. I watched them play in Cairo last spring. Brilliant. I have, of course, seen Miss Darcel in her films, but, regrettably, nothing more intimate." He smiled. "You see, Mr. Chambrun, I can be cooperative if I'm not pushed."

"It is no problem for you to tell us nothing," Chambrun said.

"I cannot invent intrigue where there is none, even to please you, Mr. Chambrun. I am here to deliver a speech to the United Nations—tomorrow if the agenda permits. When I have done so, I will be leaving for Cairo."

"You aren't concerned for your physical safety?" Hardy asked.

"My dear Lieutenant, why on earth should I be? I am here to discuss the problems relating to oil, a subject of interest to all the nations of the world. To harm me would be to inflame a situation that is already overheated. I cannot remember ever feeling quite so safe." He smiled at us as though we were not very bright children.

"You didn't know that Downing was on this floor?" Hardy asked.

"Had I seen a black coming and going I would have thought of nothing, except that when I was a child he would have been a servant and not a guest. You show me that picture." He gestured toward the magazine on the table. "Of course I have seen it before, but the faces in the background had no significance for me. The writer for the magazine, a man named Styles, I think, showed me the proofs before it actually went into print. A journalistic courtesy. But I had no reason to be concerned with Maginot's hangers-on. Only Maginot himself."

"Maginot is dangerous to you?" Hardy asked.

"Dangerous, but with his wings clipped," Ghorra said. "Every intelligence agency and police force, on both sides of the world, looks for him. He is what you might call the world's most wanted man. He has no choice but to hide." Ghorra smiled. "But even knowing that, I may say I was relieved to hear him speaking on the Algiers radio this afternoon."

"You heard him?" Chambrun asked.

"In my bedroom I have a radio that picks up channels overseas," Ghorra said. "Maginot's speech was announced well in advance. It was bloodcurdling—or would have been if I didn't know he was five thousand miles away."

"But friends here? Friends like Downing?" Hardy asked. "You're not afraid they might carry out Maginot's threats?"

A honey-sweet smile. "I count on you and your excellent police force, Lieutenant, and on Mr. Chambrun and his expert security here in the hotel."

"Then you are a damned fool," Chambrun said, "because we've had two people killed under our noses in the last eight hours. And if you won't answer questions, we have no hope of protecting you."

"I don't think you realize how safe I am," Ghorra said. "I am the seller of what everyone else in the world wants to buy—oil. If anything happens to me my people will sell to no one. Your country, your country's enemies, communists, tyrants, they are all eager to become buyers. They all protect me against the Maginots of this world. If I were to step off the curb in front of a taxi, someone would pluck me back. You say the man in the next suite has diplomatic protection? It doesn't concern me who he works for. He is almost certainly here to make sure no harm comes my way. Do not be concerned, Mr. Chambrun. I will not die in your hotel. I am in no danger of dying violently at all until after I have decided to whom I will sell. When that decision is made, I will be safely back in my own world. So do not be alarmed about me. If

Downing was Maginot's friend, ally, spy, then he was removed to make sure of my safety. I don't know by whom, you understand, and I care less. At the moment the whole world wants me safe."

"Except Maginot," Chambrun said.

"Who is hiding in some cellar in Algiers," Ghorra said. "And now, if you gentlemen will excuse me. I still haven't completed preparations for my speech tomorrow. I must get back to it."

Out in the corridor Lieutenant Hardy indulged in one of his rare explosions. "Those sonsofbitches on diplomatic passports!" he said. "They come to our town, commit any crime from a parking violation to mayhem, and we have to stand by, tip our hats, and say 'Yes, sir!'"

Chambrun appeared not to be listening. He had strolled down to the end of the corridor and stood outside the door to the Watsons' suite. I thought he was going to ring the doorbell, but he didn't.

"A twelve-year-old girl," he said to no one in particular. "Because of her handicaps she embodies the very essence of curiosity. She is in a new world, where everything begs for answers. The night before she has made a new friend."

Hardy and I watched him, and listened. When he goes off into a reconstruction like this, he is usually coming to grips with a key question. He moved slowly down the hall to the door of Suite C, Downing's rooms.

"She is bored by the clothes-choosing that involves her mother. She decides she will contact her new friend, the strange black man down the hall. She rings the bell and Downing opens the door. He is a man who has lived under the age-old prejudices of our time. There will be hell to pay if he is seen talking to this little girl again—because he is black.'' He looked at us. ''Now isn't that a monstrous world to live in? He feels warmth for the child, but he must reject her, turn her off. That must burn him. And it leaves the child confused and hurt. But there must be other things in this strange new dazzling world to explore.'' Chambrun turned toward the door of Suite B, Yvonne's second set of rooms. ''This door may be open, with the usual babblings of the French contingent going on, only the child can't hear the voices because she is stone-deaf. But an open door is an invitation, wouldn't you say? What wonderful mystery lies beyond it?''

I think I should interrupt the action here with a floor plan. All the suites on Fourteen are alike in one respect. The door from the corridor, the only way in, opens into a small vestibule. There are coat closets on either side. You can't see into the living room that lies beyond without going through the vestibule.

''Curiosity,'' Chambrun muttered to himself. ''There may be voices, laughter, angry tirades going on beyond the vestibule, but Marilyn can't hear them. There is only the open door and beyond it who knows what?''

''It could have been any room along the corridor,'' Hardy said. ''Not necessarily this one. It could have been a suite where the maids were cleaning. They'd leave the door open, wouldn't they?''

''And kill the child for interfering with their sweeping?'' Chambrun asked. ''I chose this door only because we know it is often open . . . and because Marie Orell has just finished lying to us about Downing's visit. But, yes, it could have been any other door."

"Or no suite at all," Hardy said, growing impatient. "She could have gone to the far end of the corridor. She knew about the elevators, but there was the door to the service area she hadn't explored. She goes through it, stumbles on the killer, and is clobbered."

"So let's say it could have been any door," Chambrun said, "even though I prefer this one. She goes through it and sees—what in Christ's name does she see?"

We all stood there staring at each other. We had no answer.

"What she sees requires instant silencing," Chambrun said slowly. "They don't question her, because they would have discovered she couldn't hear, couldn't speak. There she is, and—wipe-out!"

"Some kind of violence," Hardy said, "and she could identify the perpetrator."

Policemen use words like "perpetrator," right out of the police manual.

"Except that there has been no violence that we know of in any of these rooms or the service area," Chambrun said. "I am in my office when someone comes in unannounced. What could I be doing that would drive me to pick up the paperweight on my desk and crush in a child's skull? I then take the dead child, at enormous risk of detection, and stuff her into a trash can in the service area down the hall. I am caught in the act of murdering someone, dismembering someone? But what have I done with the second body?

I am making love to the wife of a prominent guest? How would the child know that it isn't legitimate? I am raping a secretary? But why haven't I been charged with rape by the victim? I am robbing the safe, but how would the child know that it wasn't my right?"

"The child knew you; you brought her flowers," I said. "A stranger would be something else, but you she would know."

"I would also know that she couldn't tell anyone," Chambrun said. "But let's face it, friends, if she saw something happen in one of these suites or in the service area, it's been completely covered up, hidden. Every suite has been serviced by the maids and Mrs. Kniffin since Marilyn disappeared. Nothing. The service area has been gone over from top to bottom by your people, Hardy. Nothing. So what, *what* did she see?"

"A psycho who takes pleasure in wipe-outs," Hardy said.

"Possible," Chambrun said, "but every instinct I have says 'no' to that. Those instincts tell me that it was one of the guests on this floor, someone we have talked to, someone who has provided you with a written statement, Hardy, which is a lie. Psycho, maybe, but someone who has a face and a name we know."

Fletcher came around the corner from the elevators. "Your secretary is trying to reach you, Mr. Chambrun," the sergeant said. "There's a man named Sandberg waiting in your office to see you."

The State Department had arrived.

THREE

WALLACE SANDBERG, one of God knows how many undersecretaries in the State Department, was a familiar type. I'd seen dozens of them, in and out of the Beaumont on United Nations business. They are tall and lanky, fiftyish, boyish with crew-cut gray hair. Some of them wear less than conservative clothes, but almost all of them wear some sort of club tie—their college tie, their regimental tie, their golf club tie. Most of them smoke pipes. The higher up they get in the department, the more ever present the pipe. When you get to be Attorney General or Secretary of Defense, the pipe is always there, even at televised press conferences. I think they think it helps to create the image of a relaxed and thoughtful man, probably kind to his dog and his mother, if he still has one. Wallace Sandberg was perfectly cut out of the pattern. He even had a nice warm smile to go with it all. His attitude toward Chambrun, at the start, was that of an old buddy-buddy.

We found him sitting in one of the green leather armchairs, a pipe between his strong white teeth while he worked on another with a pocket pipe-tool, filling one of Chambrun's ash trays with gunk from the bowl.

"Well, Pierre, you seem to have had a rather hectic day," he said. He pulled his long length up out of the chair and held out his hand. Chambrun ignored it and went around to his desk.

I introduced myself and Hardy, which gave Sandberg something to do with his hand. His handshake was firm and very sincere, I thought.

"I got the news about Luther Downing from one of my people who met me at the airport, Pierre," Sandberg said. "That, on top of the little girl, must be very distressing for you and the hotel. I know how hard you try to maintain a tranquil image."

Chambrun gave him the coldest look you can imagine. "You've come all the way from Washington to tell me something," he said. "So tell!"

"We live in a very complex world," Sandberg said regretfully. He put the extra pipe back in his jacket pocket along with the tool, and relit the one he was smoking. He sank back in the armchair and looked up at the ceiling, like a college professor about to deliver a lecture on whether Francis Bacon wrote Shakespeare's plays.

"Just facts, Wallace," Chambrun said. "No tapestry weaving, please."

Sandberg lowered his eyes to Chambrun's level. "I talked to Bowers from the airport, Pierre, so I know what you've been up to."

"I've been trying to solve two murders," Chambrun said.

"I am here to convince you that Bowers had nothing to do with either one of them," Sandberg said.

"How?"

"Just by giving you my word," Sandberg said.

"Balls, Wallace," Chambrun said. He almost never uses that kind of language, and when he does, you can depend on it you're about to be knifed. Sandberg didn't know his man too well, it seemed.

"We're old friends, Pierre. That should be enough for you, and for the Lieutenant." He gave Hardy his kindly smile.

"It's not enough for me and it damn well shouldn't be enough for Hardy," Chambrun said. "You've hired an international killer to keep an eye on Abdel Ghorra, who is about to lay a golden egg in somebody's nest. Starting with our second killing, Wallace, Luther Downing was a friend and possibly an ally of a man named Victor Maginot who would like to see Ghorra eliminated. Downing was a threat to Ghorra. Your man Bowers was out of the hotel when Downing was shot. In my book he may very well have done the shooting."

"I can only assure you that he didn't."

Sandberg, I thought, was beginning to get the message. Chambrun intended to play rough. The buddy-buddy approach wasn't going to work.

"Bowers isn't the kind of man who would let anything or anyone get in his way," Chambrun said. "Not even a twelve-year-old girl! That's why you and your chums in the Department hired him, because he won't let anything stop him. Well, I'm going to stop him, Wallace, just in case he has another killing on his mind."

Sandberg's pipe had gone out and he put it down on the little table beside his chair. "I don't think you can be allowed to play private games with the situation,

Pierre," he said. There was an unexpected toughness about the way he said it.

"It's not exactly a private game, Mr. Sandberg," Hardy said. "We have two homicides on our hands, and homicides are public business. What we know about Bowers will be in my report to the Commissioner."

"And what I know about him will be in the public press," Chambrun said. "It may not create too much of a stir, of course. The American people are sick of the Watergate story, and the CIA scandals, and accounts of assassinations in Vietnam, and Chile, and God knows where else. I will, nonetheless, feed it to them if you don't get down to something like facts!"

"Do you have any idea of the kind of pressure that can be brought to bear on you, Pierre?" Sandberg asked quietly. "I have the feeling you think you are untouchable in your little fortress here."

"When somebody else tries to use this fortress, as you have, Wallace, I will go to the mat with them—all the way."

Sandberg reached for his pipe, tamped down the tobacco with his finger, and lit it. It was an automatic with him. He wasn't even thinking about it.

"I guess you are entitled to something more than a blank sheet of paper," he said finally. Pipe smoke swirled around his gray head. "You already know more than you should know, so perhaps if I add a little to it you may be persuaded to keep the whole thing to yourself. That goes for you, too, Lieutenant. And you, Mr. Haskell."

"No promises," Chambrun said.

"So, I'll gamble on your common sense," Sandberg said. "We live in a world of cliché phrases, Pierre. We called the invasion of Cambodia an 'incursion.' We called a defeat in Vietnam 'peace with honor.' We call secret treaties 'assurances.' And we call a critical shortage of oil, on which the national security and economy depend, an 'energy crisis' which can be solved by turning down your thermostat to sixty-eight degrees. These are all phrases to make the truth seem more palatable and less frightening. The truth is that unless we can stop the Arabs from using oil as an instrument for blackmail and world control we are up the creek."

"So you use the Beaumont as a base for—"

"I use the Beaumont for nothing," Sandberg interrupted sharply. "Abdel Ghorra made his own reservations, his own plans for being here. We had nothing to do with that. But when we found out where he was staying, I called you and asked you to make space for someone on the fourteenth floor. If he had gone to the Waldorf or the Plaza, I would have made the same arrangements. It was a chance, over which I had no control and which I didn't plan, that Ghorra chose the Beaumont for his base."

"He has stayed here before," Chambrun said.

"And no one who stays here ever goes anywhere else," Sandberg said. The buddy-buddy smile that went with that didn't work. "You are surprised that we would hire Bowers—or Von Zedwitz, or Kuglemann, or whatever you choose to call him—to watch Ghorra."

"Nothing our Department does surprises me," Chambrun said. "But I am interested in the reason. This man is a wanted criminal; wanted by the law in half a dozen countries, by the old-time Nazi-fighters. He and this man Victor Maginot are birds of a feather. Wanted, wanted."

"Old adage," Sandberg said. "You fight fire with fire. Bowers is the best man there is to oppose Maginot. They play the same kind of ball game. There isn't a man in our Department, or in the CIA, or any other intelligence service who knows the European scene like Bowers. He can pick out fifty of Maginot's closest people on sight."

"Including Downing?" Hardy asked.

"Including Downing," Sandberg admitted. "But Downing wasn't dangerous in the fatal way with which we're concerned. He used words for weapons. He could write an inflammatory article, he could make a rabble-rousing speech, but he wasn't a killer. Never was. Neither Bowers nor I were concerned about his being here. You understand, there will be demonstrations outside the United Nations when Ghorra goes there tomorrow to make his speech; there will be demonstrations outside the Arab consulates, and counterdemonstrations outside the Israeli consulate. You could have expected to find Downing involved in one or all of those demonstrations. But Ghorra could have gone to the U.N. and come away without danger of any more physical harm from Downing than having a rotten cabbage thrown at him. I repeat, Downing is not—was not—a major concern of ours."

"Who, then?" Chambrun asked.

Sandberg hesitated. "Maginot and his people, of course. Maginot himself is grounded in Algiers, but his organization—?"

"So you surround Ghorra with a battalion of New York's finest; he makes his speech, you ship him off home, and nothing will have happened to him in your jurisdiction," Chambrun said. "Is that your concern? That someone will knock Ghorra off here, in the United States? Well, my concern is that someone will knock him off here in the Beaumont. I want him out, and I want your killer out."

"It's too late for that, Pierre. He's covered here in the hotel by Bowers, and we will be covered every step of the way from here to the United Nations and from the United Nations to the airport by Secret Service, police, FBI. We can't rearrange that security."

"What about the Beaumont's security?" Chambrun asked. "Explain to me what a twelve-year-old child's curiosity had to do with Ghorra and I'll know you and your killer are really on the job. I don't think you've told me anything like the whole truth, Wallace. The business of protecting presidents, visiting heads of state, is a worked-out routine that is ninety-nine percent effective. You don't have hired killers in the next bedroom to make it work."

Sandberg smiled. "How do you know?" he asked.

"Because presidents and heads of state have stayed at the Beaumont and I know who was in the next bedroom. You're not concerned with the drive to the United Nations or to the airport. You're concerned with what may happen here on the fourteenth floor of my hotel. Something has already happened. What next? So help me, Wallace, I'm going to blow this sky-high if you don't come clean with me."

Sandberg knocked out his pipe, took the second one out of his pocket, and began to fill it from an oilskin pouch. "You know," he said slowly, "that I'm not dealing with a personal problem but with a national problem."

"I know. And the name of the game is secrecy. But with two murders to deal with, Wallace, it's time to let us in on it if you care what we do about it."

Sandberg clicked his pipe stem against his teeth. "Ghorra has something to sell—oil," he said after a moment. "He is here to make a general speech about it to the U.N., but in reality he is here to listen to bids. The free world is trying to woo him; the communist world is trying to woo him. And there are others."

"What others are there?"

"Giant corporations, the multinational power houses. Let's face it, Pierre, these are people who owe allegiance to no flag, no government, no one but their stockholders. And the controlling stock is in the hands of the men at the top. Ghorra could deal with one of those corporations and suddenly, between them, they would rule the whole roost. The alternative to that—?" Sandberg shrugged. He was suddenly a very serious man. "A nuclear holocaust which would leave nothing to control and no one to control it." He leaned forward in his chair and pointed his pipe stem at Chambrun. "Is that enough to persuade you to let us play this game without interference from you or the police?"

Chambrun was carved out of rock. His eyes looked like they were made of some kind of opaque glass. "Your job is to protect Ghorra so long as he appears likely to deal with you?"

"With the free world," Sandberg said.

"Ah, yes. But if he should start to deal with the communist world, or the corporations?"

"We would have to take steps to—"

"You would kill him!" Chambrun almost shouted. "That's why you hired a man like Bowers. He can go either way for you, protect or kill. He has no convictions except about his pay check. He's sitting up there waiting for a signal from you! Ghorra is our man, so guard him. Ghorra is going their way, so eliminate him. Since killing him is at least a fifty-fifty chance, you hire a man who can't be tied to you or your department or any other department."

Sandberg just stared at him.

"Except by me," Chambrun said. "And, by God, we will connect him, Wallace, if anything more happens here or we find he's tied in to what has already happened."

Sandberg stood up very slowly, as if his muscles ached. "I'm sorry, Pierre," he said, "but we're going to have to stop you if you won't listen to reason."

I DON'T THINK the average man in the street comprehends the secret ways in which governments operate. The head man in some South American country is murdered, and we are told it is the work of leftist revolutionary factions. If it is hinted, sometime later, that the assassination may have been advantageous to some multinational corporation, some oil empire that serves us, the dead man turns out to be a leftist and his murder an act of patriotism. All actions of government, honest or evil, are wrapped up in the flag of honor.

"And sold to the man in the street," Chambrun said. "The gullibles! Us! We the people!"

We were back in his office where Lieutenant Hardy had been waiting for us. Hardy listened to Chambrun's view of what Sandberg was up to and shook his head.

"Sandberg can't commit a murder right under my nose," he said. "No one can expect I'd cover for him."

"Sandberg will turn up as innocent as Snow White," Chambrun said. "And he will find a way to stop you. You work for government and government can control you."

"And you?"

"Who knows?"

Chambrun took a cigarette from his case and lit it. The little red light on his desk phone blinked. He picked up the receiver and said, "Chambrun here." Then his lips tightened and he held out the phone to Hardy. "For you."

Hardy said "yes" several times, and then he put down the phone. He stared at Chambrun. "I have been taken off the case," he said. "I am to report to the Commissioner's office at once."

"You see?" Chambrun said dryly. "Sandberg is for real."

"They can't do anything to you, Pierre," Hardy said. "Nothing could keep me from talking."

"Those could be famous last words," Chambrun said. "There will be two words used that will keep you quiet and Mark quiet."

"Two words?" Hardy said. He was beginning to simmer.

"'National security,'" Chambrun said. "They have always worked before—at least until Watergate. They'll probably work again. By now every news agency in the country will be warned off any story I might tell."

"But not violence!" I said.

"That may depend on how persistent I am," Chambrun said. His eyes narrowed. "I'm going to find out who killed that child and hang him in public. If that exposes Sandberg's game—" He shrugged.

Hardy lumbered out of the office, muttering to himself.

Chambrun pressed the intercom button on his desk and Ruysdale answered from the outer office.

"I want Jerry Dodd here on the double," Chambrun said. "Then you, Ruysdale."

He looked at me as though I was some kind of problem. "Mark, I suggest you take your Miss Failes away from here on a few days' vacation."

"Vacation?"

"When Ghorra heads back for Egypt the day after tomorrow, the coast will clear here—to some extent."

"You're sending me away because—?"

"No point in giving them too many targets," he said.

Miss Ruysdale came in from the outer office and stood by his desk waiting for orders.

"I'm going to need you to go to Chicago for me, Ruysdale," Chambrun said. "The hotel managers' convention is there, which I can't attend. I think you could arrange for a flight sometime this evening—"

"No," Ruysdale said, and gave him a very tiny little smile.

"What the hell do you mean 'no'? I want you to—"

"You think Sandberg and his people might use me to bring pressure on you," she said matter-of-factly. "I can take care of myself, Mr. Chambrun, and I don't propose to walk out on you in a crisis just to protect my own hide. Besides, it's safer here in the hotel. We have some control over what happens here." She glanced at me. "I suppose you're trying to send Mark away, too, Mr. Chambrun."

"You've been listening at keyholes again," Chambrun said.

"I get paid for reading your mind, Mr. Chambrun," she said.

I wondered if she still called him "Mr. Chambrun" when they were alone together. I was never more convinced that there was a great deal more between them than a boss-secretary relationship. I knew then that I wasn't going to go on a vacation. I said so.

Chambrun looked at us both in a way that suggested something almost like affection. "Thanks—both of you," he said. He reached for a cigarette. "Nothing is going to happen to Ghorra under this roof. I'm going to get rid of him or I'm going to sit on him like a hen on an egg."

What he had in mind he made clear a few moments later when Jerry Dodd reported in. He gave Jerry a brief outline of what he thought Sandberg's game was. Ghorra was to be protected by Bowers as long as it appeared he might be going Sandberg's way. If, however, Ghorra seemed to be leaning another way, Bowers was to eliminate him.

"And if Ghorra is playing footsie with Sandberg, then someone else may have at him?" Jerry said.

Chambrun nodded. "So we take over the fourteenth floor," Chambrun said. "I want to put a man in Ghorra's suite with him. He can scream bloody murder, but that's the way it's going to be. If he doesn't like it, he can move somewhere else—to some other hotel. I want enough men on the floor to check every coming and going, to search every suite if necessary."

"Sandberg's evidently got the Commissioner by the short hairs if Hardy was called off," Jerry said. "The police may not like what you're planning."

"Then I'll move everybody off Fourteen—the innocent and the guilty. Send them all packing somewhere else."

"And if they don't choose to go?"

"No water, no lights, no elevator service, no food, no telephones," Chambrun said. He glanced at Ruysdale. "Inform the chief engineer. I want him to be ready in case. You, Jerry, call half a dozen men off whatever they're doing, meet me on Fourteen in ten minutes."

Ruysdale and Jerry took off. I went over to the sideboard and poured myself about four fingers of Jack Daniel's, neat.

"The hotel is crawling with newsmen and photographers," Chambrun said to me. "We're not going to be able to go to the bathroom without their asking questions. Promise them a press conference within an hour and then meet me upstairs."

I found Mike Traynor in the lobby and persuaded him to pass the word that Chambrun would meet with the press in the conference room off the lobby in an hour's time. The whole place was buzzing. I couldn't walk three yards without being surrounded by guests and other regulars who wanted to know what the hell was going on.

I finally made the fourteenth floor and found Chambrun, Jerry and five of Jerry's security people in some kind of hassle with Sergeant Fletcher, who was still on the case.

It seemed the policeman, watching the floor, reported that the Greek, Nikos Parrasis, and his bodyguard were in their suite, Bowers in his, Ghorra in his, Marie Orell and the maids still in A and B, the four bridge players having a room service supper in their two suites during a break in the tournament play downstairs, and Helen Watson was in her suite with Miss Simmons. Missing were the balance of the French contingent, Jasmine Gilhooly, and George Watson. Chambrun's problem was that Ghorra refused to answer his doorbell or some heavy knocking on the door.

"You missed him. He's gone out," Jerry Dodd was arguing with Fletcher and the policeman at the elevators.

"We didn't miss him," Fletcher insisted. "He just doesn't want company. That's his right, isn't it?"

"Pass key," Chambrun said.

Jerry Dodd has some gadget for opening locked doors that would have made him the greatest second-story man in the world. He walked down to the door of Ghorra's suite and opened the door. He went in, followed by Chambrun, the man who was going to be stationed in the suite, and me.

There was no one in the living room. The stretcher table was still littered with papers as we'd seen it a while back.

"Mr. Ghorra!" Chambrun's voice was sharp.

No answer.

Chambrun went down the hall to the first bedroom. He stopped in the doorway and we crowded up behind him. Something about the rigid set of his shoulders warned me.

He turned away, uttering something under his breath. Jerry and I wedged together in the doorway.

Ghorra was there, lying on the bed. The bedspread was bright red with blood. Ghorra looked very peaceful, even with his throat cut.

PART THREE

ONE

IT WAS epidemic.

Sergeant Fletcher, a competent officer, trained by Hardy, one of the best, was prepared to deal efficiently with the preliminaries of any homicide. He ordered us to back off, not to touch anything in the suite if we could avoid it. He used his handkerchief to cover the telephone by Ghorra's bloody bedside to call for help and the special homicide crew that would take Ghorra's rooms apart for evidence. He suggested politely that Chambrun, Jerry Dodd, and I leave the suite. These were all routines he should have followed, but I had the uncomfortable feeling that Hardy had never had the chance to bring him up to date. He couldn't know, because Hardy had had no chance to tell him, that in the adjoining suite was a man, Bowers, whose job it was either to protect or eliminate Abdel Ghorra.

Chambrun seemed not to have heard the Sergeant's request that we clear out. He was like a man in a trance, staring at the body. He seemed to be trying to force himself to see something that wasn't there to see. A weapon, for example. I thought surely he would tell Fletcher about Bowers, but he didn't. Instead he drew a very deep breath and, still trancelike, turned and walked out through the living room, through the vestibule, and out into the corridor. Jerry and I followed him.

In the hall he turned and faced the door to Bowers' suite. He spoke to Jerry, tight-lipped. "This bastard could pull a gun on us just as casually as he might light a cigarette," he said.

Jerry nodded. He took the gun he carried in a holster under his left armpit and transferred it to his jacket pocket. His hand stayed in the pocket with it.

Chambrun pressed the doorbell button.

After not too long a delay the door opened and Bowers looked out at us through his tinted glasses. I found myself staring at him for bloodstains. Nobody could have butchered Ghorra and come away clean. I could swear he was wearing the same clothes we'd seen on him earlier: the rumpled tweed jacket, the gray slacks, the plain white shirt with a knitted brown tie. There were no visible stains.

He was smiling. "Something new on the horizon, Mr. Chambrun?" he asked.

"We had a chat with your principal not too long ago," Chambrun said.

"I know," Bowers said. "He phoned me and told me. It seems you tried to play it tough with him. Sandberg doesn't look it, but he's not easy to push around. Your homicide lieutenant is aware of that, I take it."

From behind him in the living room the television set was playing. I found it hard to believe, but this professional killer had been sitting in his living room watching *Gunsmoke* when we rang his doorbell.

"Things have changed," Chambrun said. "We'd like to talk to you."

"Be my guest," Bowers said, and stood aside.

We went through the vestibule and into the living room. He followed us and turned off the TV set. "It may seem childish to you," he said, "but I have a passion for Westerns. *Gunsmoke* is a little mild, but it was the only thing at this hour."

Chambrun stood very straight and still, facing him. "What happens to you if you fail at your assignment?" he asked.

Bowers' lazy smiled widened. "I get fired," he said.

"Well, you have either just failed or just succeeded," Chambrun said.

The gray eyes behind the tinted lenses narrowed, but the smile remained. "I don't follow."

"Ghorra is lying on his bed in the next suite with his throat cut," Chambrun said. "If your job was to protect him, you've failed. If it was to kill him, you've succeeded. He's quite dead."

There was something fascinating about that moment. Bowers either had to be rocked back on his heels by the news, or he knew all about it and had to act out his surprise. He played it stone-cold, without any visible reaction of any sort for a moment. The lines at the corners of his eyes and his mouth seemed to grow deeper. That was all.

"It's not possible," he said finally, his voice very low and dangerously soft.

"It is a fact," Chambrun said. "At this moment I'm not interested in your reactions, Bowers. I want to get hold of Sandberg, and you must know how to reach him. The Ghorra ball game is over. In half an hour I meet with the press. Unless I can be convinced by him and by you that there is still some reason to keep the facts buried, I'm going to blow the whole thing sky-high."

There is one thing about Bowers. I suspect he had spent his whole life making instant decisions and he made one now.

"Sandberg's here in the hotel," he said. "You'll find him in Paul Drummond's rooms."

Drummond was a permanent resident of the Beaumont's, the executive assistant to our U.N. ambassador. Chambrun picked up the phone on the corner table and a moment later he had Sandberg on the line.

"Ghorra has been murdered," he said in a matter-of-fact voice. "I'm with Bowers now. In thirty minutes I have a press conference." He put down the phone. "He's on his way."

I glanced at Jerry Dodd. He stood there, bright-eyed, his hand still in his jacket pocket where his gun was.

Color had drained out of Bowers' face. "Sandberg told me about your theory," he said to Chambrun. "That I was to protect Ghorra as long as he seemed to be playing ball with us, that I was to kill him if he started walking the other side of the street. Interesting theory, and possibly correct. But I tell you this, that as of now my job was to protect him, and he knew it. Hell, man, I've been in and out of his suite through the connecting door a dozen times. I talked to him less than an hour ago. We had an understanding. He wouldn't go anyplace without letting me know. He wanted protection. He was glad to have me here. When I last talked to him, he was working on his speech for tomorrow. He had no plans to go anywhere tonight.''

"He didn't go anywhere," Chambrun said.

"He wouldn't have let any stranger into his suite. He wouldn't have let anyone in whom he knew might be interested in dealing with him without letting me know."

"He would have let in a maid, if a woman answered his question as to who was at the door," Chambrun said. "He would have let in a waiter, if he'd ordered food or liquor."

"He wouldn't have had to answer the doorbell," Jerry Dodd said. "We got in without any difficulty when he didn't answer. You'd know how to handle these locks, wouldn't you, Bowers?"

Bowers gave Jerry a thin smile. "Child's play," he said.

"So would any other smart operator," Jerry said. "So getting in was not such a big deal. You had the best chance, chum. There was the connecting door and he trusted you."

"When did you find out he was dealing with someone else?" Chambrun asked.

"He wasn't dealing with anyone else," Bowers said.

"So the master assassin and spy sits here watching *Gunsmoke* while Ghorra gets his throat slit from ear to ear," Chambrun said.

Bowers ignored the crack. "Parrasis and Panzer?" he asked.

"In their suite," Chambrun said.

"You talked to them? Do they know?"

"I decided to cover the most likely ground first," Chambrun said. "Meaning you."

"Who's in charge—for the police?" Bowers asked.

"Sergeant Fletcher for the moment," Chambrun said. "As soon as I talk to Sandberg I expect Lieutenant Hardy will be reassigned."

"Tell Fletcher not to let Parrasis and Panzer get away on him, whatever he does," Bowers said.

"I like your technique," Chambrun said. "We are to quickly forget about you and look somewhere else."

"Parrasis was a potential buyer," Bowers said, like a man adding up a column of figures. "If Ghorra turned him down—" He suddenly sounded angry. "Do you think if I'd killed Ghorra I'd be caught here in this room with my mouth hanging open? Do you think I'd let myself be caught here in a trap? For God sake, man, I'm a professional."

"That's a nice neat package," Chambrun said, "but I'm not ready to buy it. Because you are a professional. If you'd disappeared, everyone would know you'd killed Ghorra. Being caught here with, as you say, your mouth hanging open gives the appearance of innocence. That's the way a true professional might play it."

Bowers shook his head slowly. "You are something else!" he said.

The phone rang and Chambrun, who was still standing close to it, picked it up. Whoever it was wanted him. He listened, said "thank you," and hung up.

"Parrasis has asked the front office for his bill and for a bellboy to carry down his luggage," he said.

"Don't let him go!" Bowers said urgently.

"My dear man," Chambrun said, "no one is going to go. But no one!"

IT SEEMED that everybody wanted to go just about then. Fletcher may not have been Hardy, but he was a real tough cop. He handled what threatened to be a riot without bending an inch. Parrasis and his body-guard, Panzer, were out in the hall, surrounded by luggage, threatening to force their way out. The Greek gentleman made Yvonne Darcel's outrage sound like kindergarten hysterics. He was going, and he was going now, and nobody was going to stop him. In the middle of his tirade the quadruplets came out of their suites, headed for the evening session of the bridge championship. They looked like four related owls behind their horn-rimmed glasses. They were determined. A championship was at stake. Into this came the two French maids, mini-skirted in street clothes. It was their night off, they explained in broken English. Miss Orell tried to throw some of her lovely weight around.

Fletcher explained that there had been a murder.

"We have answered your questions, made our statements about your murders," Parrasis thundered at him. "You have no right, legal or otherwise, to hold us here." He started to wedge his way through the small mob toward the elevators.

Cops and Jerry Dodd's men barred the way.

"George!" Parrasis shouted.

Believe it or not, the mustachioed bodyguard pulled a gun. Miss Orell screamed prettily. Jerry Dodd, standing to one side, brought the butt of his own gun down on Panzer's wrist. The cry of pain from the bodyguard suggested to me that his wrist was broken. Jerry picked up the gun he had dropped.

"There has been another murder while you were all here on this floor," Fletcher explained. "No one is going anywhere until there are new questions answered, new statements made."

There was a babel of protest accompanied by little shrieks from the French maids. Only Parrasis seemed to take it in. He turned to Chambrun, who had been watching all this without comment.

"Who?" Parrasis asked.

"Ghorra," Chambrun said.

"Oh, God!" Parrasis said. He seemed unconcerned by the low moans that came from Panzer, who was hugging his injured wrist. "You've got the man who calls himself Bowers?"

"We've got everyone who was on this floor at the time it happened," Fletcher said. "And you're all staying here till we're satisfied and ready to let you go."

Just then Wallace Sandberg, the State Department genius, came around the corner from the elevators. He must have been disturbed, because his pipe was missing.

Parrasis evidently saw in Sandberg the kind of power he was accustomed to dealing with.

"You know what's happened here, Sandberg?" he asked.

Sandberg nodded.

"I am aware that this policeman is following the rules for this situation," Parrasis said. "There is no reason he should understand my position, my legal rights under a diplomatic passport. I choose to leave this slaughterhouse now. Be good enough to vouch for me."

"Not just yet," Sandberg said. "I—I don't have all of the facts yet. Bear in mind, Mr. Parrasis, that Ghorra has been murdered in my country, under our protection. I need a few hours to collect the facts before I can grant you or anyone else diplomatic courtesies." He turned to Chambrun. "Is there someplace we can talk privately, Pierre?"

There were the empty rooms that had been occupied by the late Luther Downing. When I started to follow, Sandberg objected.

"This must be private, Pierre," he said to Chambrun.

Chambrun glanced at his wristwatch. "In twenty minutes Mark is going to have to meet with the press," he said. "He'd better know what you hope he'll tell them. In any case he'll share whatever it is you choose to tell me. I have no secrets from him, or my secretary, or my security people."

Sandberg's mouth twitched in a tired smile. "You're not an easy man, Pierre."

"You don't play an easy game," Chambrun said.

We went into what had been Downing's suite and closed the door, shutting off the clamor in the hallway.

"Let's have it, Pierre," Sandberg said. He sat down in the corner of the living room couch, as though his legs weren't to be trusted.

Chambrun gave it to him without frills. "You gave me no choice except to take command of my own ship, Wallace," he said. "You had the best cop in New York called off the case. You forced me to keep Ghorra here when he was clearly a target for someone. Probably you!"

"Look, Pierre, you've got to know—"

"I know that you have a killer in the next room. There's no reason in God's world for you to have him on your payroll unless the need to kill was in the offing."

"Pierre, we don't—"

Chambrun wouldn't let him get his foot in the door. "Don't tell me what you do or don't do," he said. He was white-hot. "You all preach a very moral game down in Washington, but in the final analysis the end justifies the means. You'd knock off Ghorra just as fast as anyone else you mentioned—the communists, the big corporations, some private pirate like that Greek bastard across the hall. You all play by the same rules, or, rather, by no rules."

Sandberg was fumbling with a pipe and a pouch, but his hands weren't steady. "I can't argue ethics with you now, Pierre. How was he killed?"

"Throat cut, very efficiently. It was my intention to station one of our security people in his suite, whether he liked it or not. When he didn't answer his doorbell, we let ourselves in and found him lying in his own blood on his bed. We were too late, thanks to your screwing around with the situation."

"Bowers? Is he here on this floor?"

"In his suite. He was watching Marshal Dillon clean up Dodge City on his television set while it was happening—he says."

"Can we get him in here?"

"There are two things we do before I'll play question-and-answer with your killer or anyone else," Chambrun said. "First, you will call the Police Commissioner and get Lieutenant Hardy back on this case. He knows as well as I do that these three killings are somehow related. I don't want to waste time persuading someone else of that fact."

"The second thing?" Sandberg asked.

Chambrun glanced at his watch again. "In fifteen minutes I talk to the press like you've never heard anyone talk, unless I'm persuaded."

"The minute this story leaks all hell is going to break loose," Sandberg said. "We need time to prepare our defenses, Pierre. A few hours."

"You've got a lot of people to keep quiet," Chambrun said, waving toward the hall.

"Cut off the phone service to these suites," Sandberg said.

"After you've got Hardy reinstated," Chambrun said.

"God damn you, Pierre." But Sandberg headed for the phone.

Chambrun turned to me. "Call the switchboard from the housekeeper's room, Mark. Tell them no calls in or out to Fourteen, unless it's one of us."

The corridor was even more of a madhouse than when we'd left it. Yvonne Darcel and her two men had returned from their film showing and walked into the middle of it. The lady was adding her high-pitched French hysterics to the rest of the confusion. Fletcher, I saw, was having his trouble with the quadruplets. They were desperate to get to their championship. One of them was pleading with Fletcher to let them go down to the match. They were perfectly willing to be watched by the police. They would communicate with no one. They'd come back to Fourteen the instant the match was over.

I hesitated long enough to tell Fletcher we were cutting off phone service from the rooms and that Hardy would be back on the job. He looked relieved. By the time I got back to Suite C from the housekeeper's room, we had added someone to the cast. Paul Drummond, executive assistant to our U.N. Ambassador, had joined Chambrun and Sandberg. Drummond is a small, neat, bald little man with a very nice sense of humor and a mind like a computer when it came to U.N. affairs and personnel. I'd have a drink with him from time to time in the Trapeze.

"You're running out of time, gentlemen," Chambrun said as I came back into the suite.

"It's fairly simple," Drummond said in his crisp, unemotional voice. "We are suddenly in the center of what is called an international crisis. For the minute, Mr. Chambrun, try to believe that we had nothing to do with Ghorra's murder, in spite of the fact that we appear to have hired a killer to watch over him. If the story breaks that we had Bowers in the next suite, the whole damn world and, most particularly, our enemies, our competitors, are going to believe that we killed him to keep him from dealing with somebody else. That's what you believe, isn't it?''

"On the face of it it seems very likely,'' Chambrun said.

"If that is generally believed,'' Drummond said, "the consequences will be beyond your imagining, Mr. Chambrun. In retaliation the Arab oil people will place an embargo on their product as far as the United States is concerned, will deal with the enemy. What is cheerfully called the 'energy crisis' will become an energy disaster. It will not just affect the little man, and his car, and his electric bill. It will cripple our defenses, our navy, the air force, the army's mobility.''

"Shouldn't that have been considered before you left yourself wide open?'' Chambrun asked.

"Just for now, let's deal with the present,'' Drummond said. "Our only chance is time. Time enough to find out who killed Ghorra and make it public. He wasn't due to make an appearance until tomorrow morning when he was scheduled to make a speech at the U.N. If we can keep this undercover until then, until our hand is forced, we may have a chance. That means nobody on this floor can be permitted to tell what they already know. It means the lady who identified Bowers and spilled the beans to you must be kept, willingly or unwillingly, from telling anyone else who Henry Bowers really is. Right now we ask you to keep the press happy without adding Ghorra to their interest. Until tomorrow morning.''

Chambrun, I could see, was not buying. "Sometimes I think the curse of the world today is that it isn't run by serious men," he said. "You are stupid children playing with the lives and security of millions of people. You and Sandberg and the agency you represent hire a man who will protect or kill, according to your whims. You are mischievous children, playing spy games out of some dime novel, reveling in your cleverness. The result of your irresponsible game-playing is that an innocent child is dead, and two men have been slaughtered, and you stand here asking me to join in your mumbo jumbo. You know, don't you, that it isn't over—this senseless killing?"

The cold fury in Chambrun's voice seemed to have shaken Drummond and Sandberg.

"Ghorra was the object of everyone's interest," Drummond said. "He's dead. Of course it's over, except that getting at the truth in time may determine the next twenty-five years of our history."

"The next twenty-five years of our history don't concern me," Chambrun said. "Whatever happens, you and your counterparts will have screwed it up beyond repair. I am concerned with right now, with the next hour."

"So are we," Drummond said. "Getting at the truth—"

"The truth is too miserable, too evil, too irresponsible to matter," Chambrun said. "You will think of new games to play when the sun comes up tomorrow. All I'm concerned with is cleaning up the mess you've made in this hotel, in my private world, in an area for which I'm responsible. In the next immediate stretch of time the man who is responsible for three deaths in this hotel and *who is still somewhere on this floor* may walk out of here a free man, perhaps with your help.''

"Our help?'' Sandberg looked shocked.

"If it is Bowers, he will have your help,'' Chambrun said. "He's already getting it. You promise us he's innocent. That's help for him.''

"But I assure you—'' Drummond began.

"Don't assure me of anything, Mr. Drummond. I wouldn't believe a word you told me. If a good, tough cop like Hardy also doesn't believe you, doesn't believe someone else who's lying, if it is someone else, then the killer is going to have to find another way out. He's going to have to fight his way out, past the police, past my security people, past my helpless guests. How many more people will be killed? I know people aren't people to you, Drummond; they're just numbers. I can see you now, reporting to your superiors. 'We preserved our image at the cost of only a dozen lives. Cheap at the price.' '' Chambrun glanced at his watch. "I'm due at a press conference. Forgive me for taking so much time to tell you the kind of bastards I think you are.''

"What are you going to tell the press?'' Drummond asked in a flat voice.

"I'm not sure,'' Chambrun said. "I'll make that decision on the way down. I may not tell them what's happened up here because that could save the lives of a few dedicated reporters when our killer decides to break out.'' He headed for the door, stopped with his hand on the knob. "I'll tell you something, gentlemen. If I find out who the killer is, I may just decide to help him get away. An end to killing may be preferable to justice for the dead.''

TWO

I NEVER DID GET to attend that press conference. On the way down in the elevator Chambrun told me he was going to hold back the news of our third murder "at least until Hardy is back and in charge."

I got instructions. I was to try to locate Jasmine Gilhooly, who had left Fourteen a couple of hours back. She was probably in the Blue Lagoon. She had made it a habit to dine there each evening and to sit at her table afterwards, sipping brandy and listening to Johnny Felton's nostalgic piano. I was to warn her that discussing Bowers with anyone else could be dangerous. She was to come back up to Fourteen where the cops and Jerry Dodd could protect her—in case.

I was also to find Miss Ruysdale and give her the whole pitch from top to bottom so she'd know exactly where we stood, what was to be public knowledge and what was not. There were never any secrets from Ruysdale.

As I moved around the lobby, I was to listen. If the news of Ghorra's murder had leaked, it would be spreading around the lobby and the bars like a forest fire. If that had happened, I was to head immediately for the press conference in case he needed me. Of course, if it had leaked, that would be the first thing the reporters would ask about.

The lobby was quiet. The excitement of the late afternoon had evaporated. Guests came and went in a normal fashion, stopping at the front desk for mail or keys.

"Violence is a way of life these days," Mike Maggio, the night bell captain, said to me when I asked him how things were. "You have it, and then you forget about it like what you ate for lunch." Mike was a shrewd, city born and bred young man, with a cynical eye and ear for anything that was going on in the Beaumont. If there had been a whisper, he'd have heard it. He was still concerned about Marilyn Watson. Downing's death to him was just part of a social pattern.

"A hell of a thing for a kid's mother to face alone," he said. "Can you imagine a sonofabitch like the father?"

"Something particular about him?" I asked.

"You don't know where he is?" Mike asked.

"Among the missing," I said.

"He's not exactly missing," Mike said. "Last night he walked out on you and his wife and Miss Failes in the Blue Lagoon? Went up to the Trapeze to pour a few. Ran into Trixi Lewis."

Trixi Lewis is a high-priced hooker who turns up in the Trapeze from time to time.

"Watson went home with her," Mike said. "Turned up again, stewed to the gills, about three o'clock. A hundred bucks an hour is Trixi's price. Nothing like winning a lottery! I hear he headed back for Trixi this morning. They must have had the radio going because he came back here on the run when the news broke about the kid. As soon as the police were through with him—back to Trixi. Still there, if my spies are on the job."

His spies hadn't penetrated to Fourteen or he'd have been all over me.

I found Chambrun's old girl friend, Jasmine Velasquez Gilhooly, in the Blue Lagoon. She was sitting at her usual corner table with her usual snifter of brandy. Nine o'clock in the evening is a quiet time in the Blue Lagoon. The theater crowd hasn't come in yet. John Felton fills in between dinner and after theater at the piano. There are a whole group of middle-aged and older couples who come in once or twice a week just to listen to him, and leave when the younger, noisier crowd begins to drift in and it's time for the band and the floor show.

That night Johnny was romancing Jasmine Gilhooly with a lot of old Berlin tunes—"Remember," "Always," "What'll I Do?" She appeared to be eating it up, but evidently had her eye on the entrance because I'd only just said hello to Mr. Del Greco, the maître d', when she spotted me and beckoned me to join her.

"I was looking for you," I said as I took the chair opposite her at the table.

"It's high time somebody was looking for me," she said. Her voice, husky from booze and cigarettes, was cheerful, but I thought it covered some kind of tension. "I've been sending messages to Pierre all evening that I wanted to see him, but the miserable ingrate pays no attention. He owes me. I spotted a killer for him, didn't I?''

"Don't hate him," I said. "He's been up to his neck. He sent me to deliver a lecture and take you back upstairs."

"You have to be kidding," she said. "Pierre doesn't expect me to go back up there while Kuglemann is running around loose, does he? I have a very selfish desire to stay in one piece." She beckoned to a hovering waiter. "What are you drinking, Mark?"

"I'm afraid I haven't got time," I said.

"Nonsense. There's always time for a drink, even on the run."

I told the waiter to bring me a Jack Daniel's on the rocks. I didn't have to have my arm twisted. I felt the need.

"The fourteenth floor is about the safest place in the world just now," I said, and wondered if God would strike me dead for the lie. "There are cops, half a dozen of our security people."

"Don't kid me, buster," Jasmine said. "Who's the latest victim?"

"Downing, you mean?"

"Downing I don't mean. *Since* Downing, is what I mean." She looked at me steadily. "Play games with me, Mark, and I won't play at all."

"What makes you think there's been something else?" I asked her.

"When you get to be my age," Jasmine said, "and none of the fun is coming your way, you become a kind of perpetual peeping Tom, watching to see who else is having fun. I was in the vestibule of this place trying to reach Pierre on the phone for the umpteenth time when I saw those special homicide boys heading for the elevators. Third time today. They weren't holding a fire drill."

"New evidence," I said. I must have sounded as sour as a tenor singing a B flat when the music called for a high C, because she laughed at me.

"Who did Bowers get this time?" she asked.

Nobody was to be told about Ghorra. That was how we were playing it.

"I think Mr. Chambrun will play it straight with you if you'll come back upstairs with me to your suite," I said.

"No chance," Jasmine said. "You tell me they've got Bowers out of the hotel and locked up somewhere, with enough on him to hang him, and I might reconsider."

"They've got him surrounded," I said.

"Not good enough. I've seen him surrounded before," she said. "What is it Pierre's afraid of? That I'll blab what I know to one of these nice reporters hanging around?"

"Something like that," I said. "It's important at the moment that Bowers' real identity be kept secret."

"I'm not the only one who knows who he is," Jasmine said.

"Someone on Fourteen?"

Jasmine smiled at me. "I'll trade you," she said. "Who is the newest dead one?"

"If I tell you, you'll have to go upstairs with me and be locked in your rooms," I said.

"So there is someone!"

I was too tired and not fast enough on my feet for her.

"You're a dangerous woman," I said.

Her smile broadened. "I was. Oh, I was, Mark. Now I'm just an old bag, loaded with odds and ends of gossip. But I'll make a guess. Your latest corpse is the sheik of Araby. Bull's-eye?"

I guess I wasn't a good enough actor to hide it from her.

"Poor Pierre," she said. "The whole world is going to boil over on his living-room rug. They've got Bowers?"

"No one yet," I said.

She lit a long, brown paper cigarette with steady fingers, heavy with rings. "Pierre told me Bowers had a suite on Fourteen at the request of the State Department," she said. "That's why I'm supposed to keep my mouth shut about him, isn't it? Bowers is working for the government and he may have killed the sheik for them, right? Pierre has to take it and like it, right?"

"He won't take it lying down," I said. "There was the little girl."

"He wouldn't," she said. "But the bastards have him over a barrel. Over a barrel in the middle of a three-ring circus." She flicked the ashes from her cigarette and poured some brandy into her glass. "I said I'd trade, didn't I, Mark? So I have two little tidbits for Pierre. But I don't go back to my rooms until this is finished, settled, and done with."

"I'll tell him," I said.

She held her brandy glass in the palms of both hands, warmed it for a moment, sipped, and put it down. "I have always been interested in sexual fun and games," she said. "It was my life for a long time. Regrettably now past. But I get a vicarious pleasure watching others play at it. It so happens that Yvonne Darcel and her troop have crossed my path more than once in Europe. There is a rumor that Darcel and her double don't get along. Marie Orell, the story goes, is the real actress, cut off from a career by her unfortunate likeness to Yvonne. Yvonne, so the story goes, has it all—the career, the money, the men. Not true. The two women are as close as Siamese twins. They spend their lives playing a huge joke on their world. They share the career, the money, the men. The Yvonne Darcel that the world knows, reads about, sees on their film screens, is the invention of two accomplished schemers. Only they know which one of them is acting in a film, which one is signing autographs, which one of them is in the hay with a particular stud. A man thinks he has been lucky enough to make Yvonne Darcel, comes back for the second round, and doesn't dream he's in bed with a different woman. They die laughing at him the next day. Which one is which, even the men who live with them can't be sure. But one thing has occurred to me in the last hours. What an ideal situation for providing a perfect alibi for one of them. You and your police don't even know who you've been talking to. Was it Yvonne? Was it Marie? Who was where and when? Yvonne says she didn't see the little girl in the hall. Marie says she was in her room, dressing. But was it Yvonne who was dressing and Marie who might have seen the little girl? Yvonne Darcel is unreal. One time she is Mademoiselle X and the next time she is Mademoiselle Y. Interesting?''

''Fascinating. But so far we have no reason to think—''

''Famous last words,'' Jasmine said. ''No reason to think! So that's my number-one tidbit. My number two, on the surface, may seem more important. Nikos Parrasis knows that Bowers is Kuglemann, knows all there is to know about him.''

''How do you know that?''

''Because it was Nikos Parrasis, a very handsome and dashing young man twenty years ago, who told my husband, F.X. Gilhooly, who and what Kuglemann was. It was Nikos who warned F.X. that we shouldn't play games with him.''

''So Parrasis knows Bowers, and he knows that you know Bowers,'' I said.

''Of course.''

''I sure as hell think you better come back upstairs with me,'' I said.

''Not unless you propose to carry me bodily,'' Jasmine said. ''I'll be here till the place closes if Pierre wants to talk to me. After that I'll be in the lobby talking to the cleaning people. But I'm not going anywhere with you, Mark. Not till it's over.''

I LEFT JASMINE, smiling happily over John Felton's rendition of ''I Can Do Anything Better Than You Can,'' and detoured to the second floor, where I brought Betsy Ruysdale up to date. Extraordinary woman. You could tell her the Empire State Building had just toppled over and she'd take it as a matter of course. She was concerned over the fact that Chambrun hadn't had any dinner. Then she threw me a curve.

"Tell Mr. Chambrun the answer to the question he wanted me to ask is 'no.'"

"What question?" I asked.

She smiled at me. "He'll understand."

So I went back to Fourteen. Elevators wouldn't go to the floor, and the fire stairs were blocked off by a couple of cops who didn't know me. I had to practically produce a birth certificate to get by them.

Hardy was back and walking a very high tightrope. They'd turned Downing's suite into a sort of headquarters and interrogation room. Hardy was there with Chambrun and Jerry Dodd, being brought up to date. In the time I'd been gone the homicide boys, searching every room and every person on the floor, had come up with the weapon. It was a heavy, all-purpose Boy Scout knife, one of those gadgets with one big blade, a couple of small ones, a corkscrew and a bottle opener. The murderer had dropped it in the toilet tank in Ghorra's bathroom. Hardy wasn't hopeful that the lab would come up with any remnants of Ghorra's blood. The murderer, he thought, must have been a pretty cool operator. If he had spattered himself with Ghorra's blood, he'd taken time to clean himself up in Ghorra's bathroom before he'd risked slipping out into the hall again.

The State Department, Sandberg and Drummond, were in the next suite with Bowers.

"I'd like to think we could take all the time we need to collar our man," Hardy said. "Nice and quiet and no interference from anyone." I could tell he was still angry about the way he'd been yanked off the case earlier. "But those two bastards will weasel Bowers out of here if they have to send in the Marines to get him. Parrasis had a date with his lawyer for dinner, and that gentleman is down in the lobby screaming his head off. The manager of the bridge tournament is demanding that we turn the bridge team loose. We're wrecking his event. The French star is due at some kind of a ball and there's a committee downstairs, waiting to escort her, and demanding to know why they can't come up and get her. I don't know what kind of a snow job you did on the press, Pierre, but with all that going on they're bound to guess it was a snow job."

I broke in to tell them about Jasmine Gilhooly and her tidbits, her refusal to come upstairs, and to pass on Ruysdale's message to Chambrun that the answer to the question he'd wanted her to ask was "no." Chambrun nodded, as though the answer was entirely satisfactory.

"I wouldn't mind at all, Hardy," he said in a far-away voice, "if you moved the whole lot of them down to headquarters and held your interrogation there."

"Five minutes after I do that there'll be a dozen lawyers on hand with the documents to spring them," Hardy said. "As long as I can hold them here, with the phones not working, and no way to get to us, I can hold off a court order. It doesn't exist if it can't be served. So I take them one by one, starting with Parrasis, since he may have something new to tell us about Bowers.''

"I'm not very interested in the answers you're going to get," Chambrun said, "because nobody who matters is going to tell you the truth. But I'd like to ask you something simple before I do a little nosing around on my own."

"Something simple I might manage," Hardy said.

"The Medical Examiner's office must have made a list of the things they found on the two bodies—the little girl's and Downing's. Do you know what they found, or can you get a list for me?"

Hardy took a notebook out of his pocket. "While the Commissioner was trying to explain how helpless he is," Hardy said, "I asked that question myself. The child had almost nothing, as you might expect. Blue cotton dress, underdrawers, a sort of undershirt, blue socks, black patent leather shoes. She wasn't carrying a purse or anything."

"You said 'almost nothing,'" Chambrun said.

"In the pocket of the dress were some pictures cut out of a magazine or newspaper; pictures of herself, her mother, her father. I suppose she saw a story about the lottery and their trip to New York, and she cut out the pictures."

"Downing?"

"Brown suit, socks, and shoes. Brown silk tie. White shirt. Jockey shorts and a T-shirt. A wallet with credit cards—American Express, Master Charge, Diners'. Fifty-four dollars in bills, eighty-seven cents in change. There was a driver's license for New York

State, and a French permit. There was a paid bill from your office downstairs. There was a piece of hotel stationery on which he'd scribbled some words. The words were 'Youth is colorblind.' That's the total.''

The corner of Chambrun's mouth twitched. ''He was a poet, among other things,'' he said. ''Do you suppose he wrote those words down after his encounter with Marilyn? 'Youth is colorblind.' The basis for something he planned to work on later? The child had moved him.''

''The workings of a poetic mind, particularly a dead one, don't fascinate me,'' Hardy said. He sounded bitter. ''We have here maybe the simplest case I've ever been asked to solve. The man's throat is cut. Nobody left the floor since it happened—could have left! Fletcher we can count on. *Nobody left!* So we line 'em up in the hall, pick out the man who did it, and go home.''

''Or woman who did it,'' Chambrun said.

''Ah, yes, women's lib!'' Hardy was steaming. ''I admit a woman could have slit Ghorra's gullet, but first she'd have to get him to hold still! Let's not play games, Maestro. Bowers is our man. You know it and I know it. He was hired to do it by the august government of the United States. He had easy access to Ghorra. He was in the next suite and he admits he used the connecting door. He never had to risk being seen in the hall. That kind of thing is his business. Ghorra wouldn't have been afraid of him because he thought Bowers was here to protect him. So, no struggle. No sweat. We have only two problems. One is prove it.

Two, if we can prove it, is to avoid being shipped to Siberia before we tell anyone about it.''

"Why did he kill Marilyn?" Chambrun asked.

"You connect the killings," Hardy said. "They don't have to be connected. It could have been two other guys. A pervert kills the child. Some right-wing kook was laying for Downing. Bowers, unrelated to either killing, is on his yes-or-no assignment with Ghorra. If Ghorra jumps the wrong way, kill him. If he jumps the right way, protect him. He evidently jumped the wrong way.''

"But, as you say, prove it," Chambrun said.

As we started for the door, it opened and Wallace Sandberg and Paul Drummond came in.

"I think our man has an absolutely clean story to tell," Sandberg said. "He had talked to Ghorra about an hour before it must have happened. Ghorra assured him he wasn't going out, had to work on his speech. Bowers had nothing to worry about. He settled down to watch television. It wasn't until you told him, Pierre, that he had any reason to think anything had gone wrong.''

"I'll get Bowers' story from Bowers," Hardy said.

"The point is, Lieutenant, we want to get him out of here," Drummond said. "You're not going to be able to sit on this very long. If a reporter gets in here, a lawyer for one of the others, if Mrs. Gilhooly decides she has an interesting story to tell someone, we're in the soup. When we've got Bowers safe somewhere, we'll make him available to you.''

"You have to be kidding," Hardy said. "You take him to some diplomatically protected consulate and I can get ten warrants for his arrest and you'll just laugh at me. He's not going anywhere till I've interrogated him in my time, in my place, and I'm satisfied there's no case against him."

"You simply don't understand what it will mean if somebody sees him and connects him with us," Drummond said.

"It's already too late," Chambrun said. "Parrasis knows who Bowers is and he doesn't have to be a genius to guess who he's working for. You should thank us for cutting off his phone or the word would be out already. He must be a very happy man. His chances of dealing with Ghorra's people is a lot better than it was when you had Ghorra under your wing."

Sandberg and Drummond looked at each other unhappily.

"You'll be good enough to pass us through your guards, Lieutenant," Sandberg said. "I think Paul and I need to consult with some higher-ups."

"No chance," Hardy said. He sounded almost happy. "No one's leaving this floor till they've gone through my mill."

"Neither of us was here when it happened," Drummond said. "Walter was with me in my rooms downstairs when Chambrun called and told us. Walter came up here after Ghorra was dead, and I after that. You have no grounds whatever for holding us here."

"Oh, I've got grounds, Mr. Drummond," Hardy said. "Bowers is my number-one suspect. He was working for you. If he killed Ghorra, you are accessories to a murder."

Sandberg turned to Chambrun. "The man's an idiot!" he said. He swung around to Hardy. "Do you have any idea what will happen to you, Lieutenant, when I can get to a working telephone?"

"I've heard the threat before, Mr. Sandberg," Hardy said. "Let me see, how does it go? I'll be walking a beat on Staten Island? Is that it?"

"How long do you think you can hold us here," Drummond asked, "before they cart you off to a padded cell, Lieutenant?"

"I hope long enough for me to nail a killer to the barn door," Hardy said. He smiled at Drummond. "Along with his accomplices."

"I appeal to you, Pierre," Sandberg said. "You and the Lieutenant are playing with a time bomb. If you insist on exposing Bowers and his connection with the United States Government, you will trigger it. The consequences go far beyond anything so simple as the Lieutenant's walking a beat on Staten Island. Oh, we can get him punished. We can have financial pressures brought on you, Pierre, that will put this plush little world of yours out of business. Punishment is the simplest and the least of our needs. We need your cooperation to prevent a massive upheaval and unbalancing of critical international relations."

"You're telling me it's my patriotic duty?" Chambrun asked.

"I'm telling you just exactly that," Sandberg said. "I'm not asking you to turn a murderer loose. Bowers is innocent. Take my word for it. But we have to get him away from here before he is publicly connected."

"And if the Lieutenant and I agree to be patriotic?" Chambrun's voice told me how angry he was. I wondered if Sandberg had an ear for it, too. "How do you keep Mrs. Gilhooly quiet? And how do you keep Parrasis quiet, who is a Greek and has no patriotic impulses, who might actually find it to his advantage to tell what he knows?"

"Let us worry about that, Pierre."

"Mrs. Gilhooly is my friend with a right to call on me for help and protection," Chambrun said. "Will you send her to walk a beat on Staten Island? Will she mysteriously disappear? Will you bring financial pressure to bear on Parrasis, who may actually have more clout than you have?"

"Let us worry about them, Mr. Chambrun," Drummond said.

That was when Chambrun exploded.

"Like hell I will!" he almost shouted at them. "Our whole political system has been poisoned by people like you two with your secret deals and secret violences. You believe that the end justifies the means, which is why you had Bowers here, ready to kill if it was necessary. So Hardy and I are going to nail him if he's guilty, because we don't believe the end justifies the means."

"Oh, God, Pierre," Sandberg said. He sounded desperate.

"Maybe," Hardy said very quietly, "there is a way. Maybe your man is innocent, as you say he is. He knows everybody on this floor inside out. Maybe he sat watching television because he knew someone else was going to do his job for him. Let him point out the

killer to us and prove it, and you can take him wherever you like. I'll go that far with you."

"Get him in here," Sandberg said to Drummond.

Drummond left, almost running.

Chambrun, still white with anger, turned toward the
door himself. "I think I'd rather do my own prov-
ing," he said.

I followed him out into the hall.

"Bowers will double-talk Hardy to death," he said.

"Where do you begin?" I asked him.

"At the beginning," he said. "With a little girl who
couldn't hear or speak. Whatever Hardy thinks,
Mark, our three murders are all of one piece. I'll stake
everything on that."

Everything meant himself and his beloved hotel.

TWENTY-FOUR HOURS ago Helen Watson had been a
young woman full of joy and happy expectations. She
and her husband were suddenly rich. They were on an
Arabian Nights' adventure in the world's greatest city,
in the world's most luxurious hotel. Her handicapped
child was alive with excitement over new things to see.
There were clothes and entertainment and an un-
dreamed-of future. Just twenty-four hours ago at this
moment she and her husband had been attending a
performance of *Shenandoah*, a smash hit musical.
And then the clouds had started to roll in. There had
been her husband's angry confrontation with an old
boy friend in the Blue Lagoon, and her husband had
taken off to get himself drunk and take up with a
hooker. The next morning her child had disappeared,
to be found brutally murdered. Her husband, having

heard the news on the hooker's radio, came back to
the hotel and tried to beat her up. Now she was, in effect, a prisoner, alone with Miss Simmons, a stranger
to her, and a murderer had struck twice more. It was
all senseless, meaningless, devastating.

Shock had left Helen Watson in what seemed to be
a merciful state of feeling nothing. She smiled at
Chambrun, vaguely, when Miss Simmons let us into
the living room where they'd been sitting. Perhaps she
remembered that he had brought Marilyn flowers
during the last hours of happiness. She gave me a little nod of recognition. She sat with her hands folded
in her lap. The only sign of what must have been terrible tensions was the whiteness of her knuckles. Her
hands were interlocked, vise-tight.

What do you say? "How are you?" She might, for
God sake, tell you!

Chambrun is Chambrun. He didn't bother with any
minor politenesses.

"I need to ask you some questions about Marilyn," he said.

A nerve twitched high up on her cheek, but the fixed
smile remained.

"Did she enjoy cutting pictures out of newspapers
and magazines?" Chambrun asked.

The question obviously surprised Mrs. Watson.
"How did you know?"

"When they found her," Chambrun said, "she had
some pictures of you and your husband and herself in
her pocket—cut out of a newspaper or magazine, I
suppose."

"She thought of them as some other children might think of dolls," Helen Watson said. "At home there are boxes full of them."

"But she did some cutting out here?" Chambrun asked.

The woman frowned, as if it took enormous concentration to remember. "I—I was rather cross about it," she said. "God help me, it was almost the last—the last thing between us."

"Would you tell me about it?"

"It—it was this morning, I think. I—I've lost track of time in a way, Mr. Chambrun."

"I understand," he said.

"Miss Failes had come that morning—this morning. With the clothes. We—we went into the bedroom because there was a full-length mirror there, leaving Marilyn in here. I tried on a dress. It—it was lovely. I remember I ran out here to show Marilyn. She was sitting on the floor with a magazine and a pair of scissors. She was cutting pictures out of it. She—she seemed pleased with the dress, but she was more excited by the pictures. There were some of us, and some others."

"Do you know what others?"

"I didn't look at them, Mr. Chambrun. She always cut out pictures of people she thought were attractive, handsome. As I told you, they were dolls she liked to play with. This was one of the news magazines that carried a story about our winning the lottery, and there were pictures of us taken by one of their photographers when we were still in Carlton's Creek.

I was annoyed with her because the magazine wasn't ours.''

"How do you mean?''

"It belonged to the hotel, Mr. Chambrun. It was one of several magazines left here for us. They weren't ours, and I tried to convey to her that she shouldn't have cut things out of the one she had. She was hurt because—because she saw that I was displeased.'' For just an instant I thought she was going to break. "I went back to try another dress, and—and that was the last time I saw her.''

Chambrun stood very quietly looking down at her. "You don't know what other pictures she had cut out besides the ones of you all?''

"I didn't look. It didn't matter, did it? It was just the act itself that mattered.''

"The magazines were yours, of course,'' Chambrun said. "She could have done anything she pleased with them. Is the cut-up magazine still here, Mrs. Watson?''

She looked around vaguely. "I—I think the maid took it when she emptied the wastebasket later that morning.''

"But it was a news magazine?''

"I remember that because our pictures were in it. That was the only magazine that covered the lottery story with pictures. *Today* I think it's called.''

"Fine. We shouldn't have any trouble locating another copy of it,'' Chambrun said. "Tell me, Mrs. Watson, could Marilyn read?''

Her eyelids fluttered closed. "She was a terribly bright child, Mr. Chambrun, in spite of her problems. Yes, she could read in a very limited way." She looked up, almost apologetically. "Concrete objects—a table, a chair, a book, food, a bridge, an automobile. I taught her to match the printed or written word with an object. Abstract things weren't possible. Some things like 'pain' or 'love' I was able to convey—oh, my God!"

Chambrun waited a moment for her to regain control. "What about names?" he asked.

"Oh, yes, where they were names of people she knew. 'Helen'—and I would point to me. 'George'—and I would point to George. If it was you, I would write 'Chambrun' and she would recognize it. It wasn't a matter of pronouncing it, you understand. But the written name, when it had been connected to someone she'd seen or knew, she could read. We—we had no trouble communicating with her about simple things."

"I'd like to change the subject, Mrs. Watson," Chambrun said. "Were you upset when the baby sitter told you about Marilyn's contact with Luther Downing?"

"Yes—at first. You see, the sitter implied that the black man had made the move toward Marilyn. But—but when I thought about it I realized it must have been Marilyn. There are no blacks in Carlton's Creek. I don't know that she ever had any close contact with a black person. I knew how curious she was, how fearless, how eager to investigate something strange. I guessed it must have been Marilyn who approached Mr. Downing. That the sitter had it wrong."

"I think she must have," Chambrun said.

"How terrible that he was shot!" Helen Watson said.

"We found something on him after he died, too, Mrs. Watson," Chambrun said. His eyes had narrowed and I could see he was thinking way beyond the moment. "He had written some words on a piece of paper. 'Youth is colorblind.' He was a poet, you know. I think Marilyn's friendly approach, her obvious pleasure with his looks, must have moved him. I think—" He let it drift away, seemed to come sharply back to the present. "I'm sorry to have to distress you with questions, Mrs. Watson. I hope this will all be over soon, with answers that will at least save us the pain of wondering any longer."

In the vestibule he told Miss Simmons he was sorry to leave her there, but he had no alternative.

"I don't mind," Miss Simmons said. "That iron control is going to break any time, Mr. Chambrun, and she shouldn't be alone when it happens."

Out in the corridor Chambrun turned to me. "I want a copy of *Today*."

"There should be one in each of the rooms on this floor," I said. It was standard practice to have several magazines left in each room in the hotel, usually a current news magazine, *Cue*, which lists all the entertainments—theaters, movies, music, and the like, and a *New Yorker*.

"Jasmine's suite is empty," Chambrun said.

I got the pass key from the housekeeper's room and we went in to Suite J together. It smelled female in there. The lady still wore a very seductive perfume. The magazines that had been left in J were stacked on a side table untouched. I got Chambrun the copy of *Today* and looked over his shoulder as he thumbed through it. There was the picture story of the Watsons; there was a story of a Vietnamese family who were working on a farm in Oregon; there was a story on a Western Senator who might be a Democratic candidate for the presidency in the November elections; there was a story of a terrorist raid on an airport in Saudi Arabia with pictures of a burning control tower and, in an insert, a picture of our old friend Victor Maginot, smiling and waving at someone out of the camera's range. The story indicated that Maginot was suspected of masterminding the raid.

Chambrun's voice was almost a whisper. "He would have made a very handsome doll for Marilyn," he said. He looked at me, and his eyes were very bright. "I would have bet next year's salary we'd find a picture of Maginot in this magazine."

"Why?" I asked. "What reason could you have—?"

"Because I think Maginot is here, in this hotel, on this floor. I think he is our killer."

"But he's in Algiers! He was on the radio there this afternoon!"

"Not so," Chambrun said. "The message you brought me from Ruysdale? I asked her to contact a friend of mine in Algiers with a question. Did Maginot make his speech today in person, or was it taped? The answer was 'no,' he did not make it in person. He could have been anywhere. I think he was—I think he is—here!"

"Isn't that reaching?" I asked. "We couldn't mistake him, we couldn't miss him. He's too distinctive. Someone said he's like a glamorous movie star. Look at him!"

"I think Marilyn looked at him, which is why she died," Chambrun said.

"That's too far out!" I said. It just didn't make any sense to me. Maginot couldn't be here on this floor. There was no place he could hide. The police and Jerry's people had covered every inch of space, had talked to everyone, accounted for everyone. There had been no new face on the scene, no new personality in the cast of characters.

"Maginot could afford to let no one except his close associates know that he was here. Until he had done what he came here to do he couldn't afford to have anyone know. He's wanted in a dozen places. The child stumbled on him, had his picture in her hand, points to him, points to the picture, is about to tell all she knows and has seen—he thinks. He doesn't stop to find out that she is deaf and dumb. He silences her—forever. He had to, he thought, if he was going to carry out his mission."

"It's too much," I said.

"It's only the beginning of it," Chambrun said.

THREE

I HAVE FOLLOWED Chambrun before into what seemed like a fantasy world of his. I have seen him apparently ignore evidence and jump to a conclusion that seemed to be based on sheer dreaming, only to see him look back and casually drop all the pieces into place. This Victor Maginot theory seemed totally unreal to me, but Chambrun was my man. "Mine not to reason why—"

I got my orders. I was to attempt the unlikely job of finding the magazine from which Marilyn had cut her pictures in a mountain of hotel trash. It was just possible that the trash from the fourteenth floor had not been tossed into the main collection. It was important, I was told. I was to get a couple of Jerry's men to help, and once they were on the track, I had another job to do. I was to show the picture of Maginot in *Today* to Dakin, the head man of the hard-hats who had been picketing the hotel. He was to circulate it on the chance that someone may have gotten a glimpse of the man who shot Downing. We just might get an identification.

"Are you saying that Maginot shot Downing?" I remember asking Chambrun. "For God sake, boss, Downing was his friend!"

"Downing was a friend who objected to the murder of a little girl who had touched his face with pleasure, who was colorblind."

Oh, Jesus, I thought, the Great Man has gone off his rocker.

I was to tell Jerry Dodd, *but nobody else*, what Chambrun believed. If Jerry knew, there might be something he had seen or heard that hadn't made sense that might make sense in this context.

We had one piece of luck. The trash from Fourteen was still in the barrels from that floor. I left Jerry's men fumbling around in piles of old Kleenexes, cigarette ashes, and God knows what else to find a cut-up magazine. I had no idea how to reach Dakin, the hard-hat, but Mike Maggio, the night bell captain, thought he could manage it for me. He took the instructions, asked no questions. That was our Mike.

I found Jerry Dodd in his office, looking like a man who hadn't slept for three days. There were other areas of security he had to cover in addition to what was happening on Fourteen. He listened, shaking his head from side to side as I talked, staring at the picture of Maginot in *Today*.

"This guy isn't on Fourteen now," he said positively. "He hasn't been there since the child was killed. Whether he was there before we found the girl I have no way of knowing. But not since we found her."

"Disguised?" I suggested.

"You think after twenty years in the business I can't spot a guy who's wearing a false mustache?" Jerry asked, impatient. "I tell you—and the boss—this Maginot character isn't on Fourteen now."

"The boss says he is."

"I wish he wouldn't," Jerry said, "because the sonofabitch is always right."

I knew how he felt. It was how I felt. "You got a message for him?" I asked.

"I'll be back up there on the double," Jerry said. "I have to reassign my people. So many of them working on the Fourteen job. We're spread thin."

I was aware, when I headed for the second floor, how great the tensions must have been up on Fourteen. I felt free, released; I didn't want to go back. I wanted to find myself busy with little piddling things. Not to tell anybody didn't mean not to tell Betsy Ruysdale; she was Chambrun's right arm, the left lobe of his brain. She already knew about his Maginot theory. She'd made the telephone call to Algiers for him.

Ruysdale wasn't in her office, so I went on into Chambrun's holy-of-holies. She wasn't there either. It wasn't like her to leave the offices open and unmanned. Then I realized that she was human like anyone else. She was probably in the john. She had a little powder room of her own opening off her office. I lit a cigarette and waited, fidgeting. I figured after a while she must be reading a very long novel. I went over and knocked on the powder room door. No answer. I persuaded myself she could be ill, could have fainted. I tried the powder room door. It didn't resist. Ruysdale wasn't there. I knew she'd be back in a moment or two or she'd have locked the offices.

That second floor, or mezzanine, at the Beaumont is, relatively, a family affair. There is Chambrun's suite of offices, the telephone switchboards presided over by half a dozen operators and a supervisor, my apartment, the accounting office which had people working adding machines and computers around the clock, and the public relations offices. I figured Ruysdale was in the switchboard quarters, probably talking to Mrs. Veach, the chief operator and night supervisor. With all the phones on Fourteen being monitored—I thought I would cheat just a little before I ran her down. In my apartment Carol Failes had been waiting for me for what must have seemed like a lifetime to her.

I unlocked my apartment door and went in, prepared to be embraced and scolded. No Carol. I looked around for the note she must have left telling me she had gone to her own place. She hadn't left a note. She must, I thought, be angry. I picked up my phone and gave the switchboard operator I got Carol's home phone number.

"And, by the way, is Miss Ruysdale in there with you?" I asked.

"No, she isn't, Mr. Haskell."

I waited, frowning, as Carol's number rang and rang. She couldn't be that angry, I thought. She had to know I'd been hung up. Perhaps she'd gone out somewhere for something to eat.

Ruysdale, I told myself, had to be in the accounting office. There's only a skeleton crew there at night, two girls pecking away at adding machines as checks from the restaurants and bars that were to be charged came up and telephone slips from the switchboard. Ruysdale wasn't there and hadn't been there. There was no point in looking in the P.R. offices for her. They'd been locked up since five o'clock. It was, my watch told me, now going on ten.

The chances were, I thought, that Ruysdale had gotten back to her office while I was trying to get Carol on the phone in my apartment. I went back down the hall.

No Ruysdale.

I think it was then that I felt a small knot tightening in my gut. It was unthinkable that Ruysdale would have left Chambrun's suite of offices unlocked and open for so long, inviting anyone to prowl, or steal, or God knows what.

Mrs. Veach, the switchboard supervisor, a hard-faced but pleasant lady, had nothing to offer on Miss Ruysdale's absence.

"There haven't been any unanswered phone calls to the office or they'd have been reported," she told me. "What's going on up on Fourteen, Mr. Haskell? We must have turned away a hundred calls."

"We're trying to pin the tail on the donkey," I told her.

The lobby was busier than when I'd last been there. The theater crowd was beginning to drift back, headed for the Blue Lagoon and the Trapeze. I checked with the people at the desk and a couple of the bellhops on the floor. None of them remembered seeing Ruysdale, or Carol, for that matter.

The knot in my gut tightened.

I took an elevator to Thirteen and talked my way past the cops on the stairway to get up to Fourteen. The doors to A and B were open and I could hear the

French people jabbering at each other. I found Chambrun and Hardy in the suite that had been Downing's, along with the two State Department characters and the mild-mannered assassin, Henry Bowers—or Kuglemann, or Von Zedwitz.

Chambrun had sprung his theory on them, and it had been received in a variety of ways. Sandberg and Drummond were delighted with it. It meant their man was in the clear, they could spirit him away, their malevolent secret kept. Hardy was skeptical, in spite of a minor bit of supporting evidence. The men who had searched the trash had come up with the cut-up copy of *Today*. Sure enough, Marilyn Watson had snipped out the picture of Victor Maginot.

I couldn't tell what Hardy thought. His eyes, shaded by his tinted glasses, looked blank.

"There is only one thing I can tell you, Mr. Chambrun," Bowers was saying as I came into the room. "There is no such thing as the impossible. You say Maginot is still somewhere on this floor because there is no way he could have left. I say he could have left."

"How?" Chambrun asked his voice sharp.

"I haven't the faintest idea," Bowers said. "But nothing is impossible. I will tell you something else. I know Victor Maginot personally. He once hired me to do a job for him." A faint smile. "Oh, yes, I work for all kinds of people, Mr. Chambrun. But I know Victor as well as I'd know my brother, if I had one. My brother couldn't hide from me behind a disguise. Neither could Victor. I never saw Victor on this floor or in this hotel at any time since I've been here."

"That doesn't mean he wasn't and isn't here," Chambrun said.

"No, it doesn't. But let me tell you, if I had seen him, I wouldn't have been sitting in my suite watching television. I would have been standing over Ghorra with a gun in my hand, ready to protect him. Because Victor could only have had one reason for being here—to get Ghorra."

"Or your orders could have changed," Chambrun said, "and you could have been chuckling to yourself as you watched Marshal Dillon clean up Dodge City, happy in the knowledge that someone else was going to do your dirty work for you without even being asked."

"That's simply not so, Pierre," Sandberg insisted. "We had every reason to be sure Ghorra was going to play his cards our way."

"Had that been so, I'd have arranged to be a long, long way from here," Bowers said. "What better chance for me to be absolutely clear of any suspicion?"

It had a ring of truth to it. I wanted to get Chambrun aside and tell him about Miss Ruysdale's unexplained absence but he was under a full head of steam. He was fascinated with his own invention, I thought.

"I've said before that I suspect coincidences," he said. "You told us, Bowers, that Yvonne Darcel came out of some flesh palace in Marseilles. I knew Victor Maginot's father. He was shot down in the streets of Marseilles. Victor Maginot was raised in Marseilles. Does that suggest anything to you? It does to me—the strong possibility that Yvonne Darcel and Victor Maginot know each other, are friends, lovers, co-conspirators."

"A guess, of course," Bowers said. "I never heard of their being connected in any way."

"Some people have the delicacy to keep their sex lives private," Chambrun said. "Let me paint a picture for you, gentlemen. A little girl cuts out photographs in a magazine. They are like dolls to her. One of them is the photograph of a handsome man—a Prince Charming. She puts the cutouts in the pocket of her little cotton frock and wanders out into the hall. Her mother is busy in the next room. The child is bored, eager for a new adventure. She knocks on the door of the suite where her newly found black friend lives. He turns her off, sends her away. Who knows, perhaps he watches her through a crack in the door as she proceeds on down the hall—to an open door, the door to A or B. The open door invites her in. She can hear nothing, so if there are conversations they are not in her consciousness. She walks through the empty vestibule to the living room and there, by all that's holy, is Prince Charming. Perhaps he is embracing the glamorous movie star. Wild with excitement, the child takes the photograph of the man out of her pocket, holds it out to show him, tries to communicate with excited gestures. Victor Maginot knows that the child has identified him, that if she goes away and tells someone, his game is ruined. And so—" Chambrun shrugged. He brought his right fist down into the palm of his left hand. "It is an instinctive act of self-preservation."

"How could Maginot have gotten up there in the first place without risking being seen?" Hardy asked.

"No one was looking for him. He was in Algiers, wasn't he? Nothing had happened here in the hotel. People came and went to and from the movie stars' suites of rooms. The press, fans, autograph hunters. All Maginot needed was a soft hat with the brim pulled down."

"But why would he risk it?" Hardy asked.

"Hunger for his lady love," Sandberg suggested.

"More likely to get an exact lay of the land," Chambrun said, "and to provide for a place to lie in wait until the right moment came. Yvonne may be his love, but certainly she and her people knew why Maginot was here. They were prepared to help him."

"Are you suggesting he may be hiding in their rooms now?" Drummond asked.

"Not possible," Hardy said. "We've searched every room, every toilet, every closet, every cupboard on this floor."

"Then is he disguised as Martine, the husband, or Nelson, the other girl's lover?" Sandberg asked.

"The child wouldn't have recognized him if he'd been disguised," Chambrun said.

"Besides, I have known Martine and Nelson by sight for some years," Bowers said. "They are themselves. They are for real."

"How did they dispose of the child's body?" Hardy asked.

"I can tell you a part of how," Chambrun said. "Yvonne raised a commotion about missing towels in Suite B—towels she had herself removed. She sum-

moned Mrs. Kniffin and the maids. While she en-
gaged them, the only people likely to be wandering
around the hall, in an hysterical tirade, someone took
the child's body to the service area and jammed it into
the trash barrel. But I suggest we ask them exactly how
they managed it.''

Hardy drew a deep breath. "Why not?" he said.

As he and Chambrun started to leave, I managed to
stop my man in the vestibule and tell him about Miss
Ruysdale's unexplained absence from the office. He
stood very still for a moment, staring straight at me.

"Unlike her," he said.

"Damned unlike her," I said.

He reached out and put his hand on my arm.
"There's probably a perfectly reasonable explana-
tion," he said. "Tell Jerry Dodd to find her, Mark! He
is to drop everything else. Ruysdale comes first."

"If you're thinking what I'm thinking, that may not
be so easy," I said.

His hand gripped my arm so tightly it hurt. "If
anything has happened to her—" He didn't finish
saying what would happen.

I GOT THROUGH to Jerry Dodd on the telephone in the
housekeeper's room after being quizzed by Mrs. Veach
to make certain I was who I said I was.

"It's hard to believe she could have left the hotel, or
been forced to leave it, without being seen," Jerry
said. "Everybody on the staff, top to bottom, knows
her and would notice her. Tell the boss to keep his
cool. I'll find her. Probably some simple explana-
tion."

"Probably," I said.

"Yeah, probably," Jerry said, and I knew he doubted it as painfully as I did. Betsy Ruysdale, in a crisis time, wouldn't let herself, willingly, become unavailable to Chambrun.

By the time I got back to Suite A, Hardy was only just managing to put an end to a shouting match in which the explosive Yvonne had threatened to sue the city, sue the hotel, and personally eviscerate anyone who kept her shut up in 'this goddamned place' a minute longer. I kept wondering, in view of what Jasmine Gilhooly had told me, which one of the two girls was Yvonne at this moment. Mademoiselle X or Mademoiselle Y? The other one, whichever, Martine and Nelson, and the two maids made up a background for the star performer. I thought they seemed a little less relaxed than the last time I'd seen them. No caressing of thighs. That could be natural. It had been a long, nerve-fraying day for everyone.

"Enough!" Chambrun suddenly shouted.

It was so unexpectedly explosive that Yvonne stopped in the middle of a sentence, her mouth, quite literally, hanging open.

"I've had all of this show-business routine I propose to take," Chambrun said, his face white with anger. He would have scared the hell out of me if I'd been in their shoes. "I am going to tell you all what I know," he said. "Then I will ask you some questions. If you answer them with the truth, you may hope for some kind of mercy from us, because the truth may help us to put an end to this horror—pos-

sibly save another life." His voice shook a little, and I
suspected he was thinking of Ruysdale.

"There is nothing we know that can be of any
help," Yvonne said.

"I'll tell you what you know," Chambrun said.
"Sometime before eleven-fifteen this morning, Victor Maginot came to call on you, you or the other girl
there who may have been 'Yvonne' this morning."

"I do not know who any Victor Maginot is,"
Yvonne said.

"You know who he is. Every Frenchman knows
who he is: a sort of folk hero. You—or the girl who is
sometimes you—grew up in Marseilles with him. I
submit that you—or the other girl—are or have been
his lover. If not, that you believed in his cause and
were willing to help. All of you!" His eyes swept the
suddenly tense faces behind Yvonne. "He came here
this morning because he needed your help. His aim, as
he has announced publicly, was to assassinate Abdel
Ghorra. He came here to your suite to discover just
what the layout is on this floor, to plan with you how
he could hide here until just the right moment came
for him to strike at his enemy."

"Monsieur Chambrun, I tell you—"

"Don't tell me anything yet, Yvonne. I haven't
asked you anything yet. While he was discussing things
with you, the little girl from down the hall, Marilyn
Watson, suddenly appeared here in this room. She had
a picture of Maginot in her hands. She was clearly excited. Maginot saw his whole plan falling apart. If the
child told anyone she had seen him, he was done for.
He didn't know that she was deaf and dumb. She had

to be silenced—and he silenced her. While you watched!"

The room was dead silent for a moment. Even Yvonne failed to protest.

"What to do with that innocent child's body? It couldn't be left here in your suite. People would be looking for her soon. How to take it out, with the maids and the housekeeper busy in the corridor and coming and going from the other suites? For an improvisation your plan was good, mademoiselle. You called the housekeeper and the maids to the next suite with a complaint. Something about linens. While you were chewing them out, Maginot, perhaps with help from Mr. Martine or Mr. Nelson, carried the little girl's body out to the service area and stuffed it in a trash barrel. That was murder number one, and I think you will all be judged accomplices."

"But I tell you—"

"Not yet, because I haven't finished telling you," Chambrun said. Chambrun, the hanging judge. It was fascinating to watch them all, because he had them hypnotized like a snake with a bird. "If Maginot had planned to stay here, hidden until the right moment came, he had to change his plans. People might come here looking for the child. He would have to go and come back another time, later on. There was no one to stop his going at that time." Chambrun hesitated for a moment. Then he went on. "But the little girl had been responsible for a further disaster, quite unwittingly. Across the hall from you, mademoiselle, was Luther Downing, the black poet. He was a friend and supporter of Maginot's. He believed in Magi-

not's cause. And he saw Maginot when he came here
this morning. I don't know whether Maginot knew it
or not. It didn't matter. The secret of his being here,
in this hotel, in this country, was perfectly safe with
Downing. Downing would never turn him in, even if
he guessed why Maginot was here. But something
happened that made Downing a dangerous man to
Maginot. Downing had had an encounter with the little girl the night before, an encounter that moved him,
touched him. This morning the child came to his door
and he sent her away, for reasons that aren't important to you. He watched her go, through a crack in his
door, and saw her come in here, where he knew Maginot was with you.

"Later word spread that the little girl was missing.
People were questioned. You in this suite denied having seen her, but he knew she had been here. Much
later he heard that she had been found dead, murdered, thrown away like old garbage. And he guessed
what might have happened.

"When it was possible, he came here to see you—
one of you. Not to ask for an autograph as we were
told. You didn't drive him out of here in outrage as we
were told. He demanded to know what had happened, if you were responsible for the child's murder.
He was deeply angry and you recognized how dangerous he might be to Maginot. The only person to handle it was Maginot himself. I suspect you knew how to
reach Maginot, let Downing talk to him on the phone.
We'll be able to check that on the phone slips. Maginot persuaded Downing to meet him somewhere in
about an hour. Downing was willing to let Maginot

speak his piece, but the murder of the little girl was too much for him, and Maginot sensed it. He was waiting outside the hotel when Downing set out to keep his appointment, and he shot him to death. That was murder number two, and I think you will all be judged accomplices in that."

I heard the man Paul Martine mutter a soft prayer in French. They were all like frozen statues.

"Now," Chambrun said, "after Downing was murdered, this floor was sealed off. Nobody could leave. Nobody could return from the outside except the people who were registered here. There was no way for Maginot to get back here, mademoiselle. And yet he did, and committed a third murder."

"Unless one of you, his friends, undertook to do the job for him," Hardy said, speaking for the first time. "No, no, no!" Yvonne said.

"How did he get back up here?" Chambrun insisted.

"Before God, Monsieur Chambrun, I do not know!" Yvonne said.

"It is your one chance to spend less than the rest of your lives behind prison bars," Chambrun said. "Tell us how he got here and where he is."

"Look here, Mr. Chambrun, isn't it our right to have a lawyer present?" the man named Chip Nelson asked. "Don't the police have to read us our rights before they question us?"

"The police haven't questioned you yet, Mr. Nelson. I am not the police. But I promise you I am the avenging angel for three murdered people. I advise you to tell me what I want to know. Where is Maginot?"

At that moment Jerry Dodd came through the vestibule and into the room. One look at his face was enough for me. He knew something. He beckoned to Chambrun, and Chambrun and Hardy and I went out into the hall with him, leaving the French contingent to figure out their futures.

"Ruysdale?" Chambrun asked.

"I haven't found her," Jerry said in a flat, dead-sounding voice. "But I have a message for you. It came over an outside phone. You are to let everyone on this floor leave the hotel, unmolested by you or the police, or you won't see Miss Ruysdale or Miss Failes alive again."

"Carol?" I heard myself say.

Jerry glanced at me. "That's the message," he said.

IF CHAMBRUN was shaken by that message, he gave no outward sign of it. He had that look of intense concentration on his face that you might see on the face of a chess player whose opponent has just made an unexpected and dangerous move.

"How far has your search for Ruysdale gone, Jerry?" he asked.

"Far enough to convince me that she hasn't left the hotel," Jerry said. "Far enough to convince me that she hasn't used an elevator to go anywhere above the second floor. Far enough to convince me that she hasn't been in the lobby or any of the public rooms. Far enough to convince me she didn't go out through the cellars."

"And not escorted out by some gent who had a gun in her ribs?" Chambrun asked.

"Not Miss Ruysdale," Jerry said. "The Failes girl I can't vouch for. I wasn't looking for her or asking about her. Didn't know she was involved until I got the message on the phone. Male voice. Muffled—like a handkerchief held over the mouthpiece."

"Why Carol?" I asked.

"Bad luck, I'd guess," Chambrun said. "You'd kept her waiting a long time, Mark. She probably walked down the hall to ask Ruysdale if there was any word from you and stepped into the middle of a kidnapping. Tough for her."

"Maginot has friends on the outside as well as the French group here on the inside," Hardy said.

"Oh, he's not a lone wolf, Lieutenant. He has a big following. He's the leader of a revolution." Chambrun's lips moved in a tight little smile. "There are plenty of people all over the world, in every big city, ready to answer his call for help. But he has just given himself away. The problem is how to handle him without endangering Ruysdale and Miss Failes."

"Given himself away?" Hardy asked, scowling. "How the hell has he given himself away?"

"The message, of course," Chambrun said impatiently. "We are to let everyone on this floor walk away unmolested. But we will be watching even if we make no effort to stop them."

"So we see him and we just let him go?" Jerry asked.

"So we see him—if we have the eyes to see him with," Chambrun said. "We saw him come in, but we didn't stop him. Now we'll see him go out. But this time—"

"Will you for God sake stop the double talk," Hardy said.

"He isn't Martine or Nelson," Chambrun said. "He isn't Parrasis, a world figure. He isn't Panzer, Parrasis's bodyguard, whom Bowers has known from way back. He isn't Bowers or Sandberg or Drummond. That leaves the bridge team."

"Internationally known, in the public eye all over the world," Hardy said.

"But four anonymous look-alikes," Chambrun said. "Can you put a name to one of them? Who is that? I ask, pointing. And you say, 'That's one of the bridge team.' You don't give me a name. Conservative haircuts, conservative tweed jackets, conservative flannel slacks, owlish horn-rimmed glasses. The quadruplets! Not alike, but alike. We think of them as four, not as individuals. That's how Victor Maginot got up here to assassinate Ghorra. The supper break came at the tournament downstairs. Maginot, properly dressed for his role, took the place of one of the quadruplets—probably changed places in the men's room downstairs. The plan—they would come up here for a room service supper. Your man Fletcher is checking all the comings and goings. He's a good man, Hardy, but he did what you might have done, what I might have done. He checked each person who came and went—he looked at a face, he checked a name. But with the quadruplets he looked, saw that there were four of them, and passed them in."

"Oh, wow!" Jerry said.

"It was really quite a brilliant plan," Chambrun said. "They had the next suite to Ghorra. There is a connecting door, locked of course. But as you know, Jerry, and as Bowers pointed out, it would be child's play for a professional to open it. Maginot opens the door, slips in, cuts Ghorra's throat, cleans himself up in Ghorra's bathroom, and rejoins the bridge players. They have reason to hope that no one will find Ghorra until it's time to return to the tournament. Maginot will walk out, quite calmly, past Fletcher, who will count up to four again. Downstairs the real bridge player will take his place and Maginot will be gone, free as a bird. Only this was a very bad day for Maginot, a day in which little things went wrong—first the child who just wandered in, then Downing who saw and guessed, and finally the unlucky, for him, discovery of Ghorra before the dinner break was over."

"All of this assumes that the bridge players were willing collaborators," Hardy said.

"Bowers told us the bridge playing was a cover for criminal activities," Chambrun said. "Maybe they were willing, maybe Maginot has something on them. We live in the age of blackmail—blackmail by terrorists and hijackers, blackmail by governments, blackmail by psalm-singing men in high places. We are, ourselves, at this moment being blackmailed by an assassin. We let him walk out, free and clear, or the blood of people we care about will be spilled."

"So we submit, as everyone else submits?" Hardy asked.

"I told you long ago I would be willing to let the killer go if it would stop the killings," Chambrun said. "I was talking then about the possibility of his trying to shoot his way out. I would let him go now if I could be certain the women would be released. But how can I be certain of that? They have seen the people who abducted them. Maginot can't guarantee their behavior."

"But the only chance is to let him go," Hardy said. "We have to risk it."

"It's the new world, the new way," Chambrun said bitterly. "Innocent people's lives used to bargain for evil. Well, perhaps we can match evil with evil."

I didn't know what he was talking about at the time, but later I understood. Chambrun was going to do something he considered evil.

IT HAPPENED like this.

There were instructions that set my heart pounding against my ribs. Hardy and Jerry Dodd both took off and I realized that Chambrun and I were about to face a killer who would be desperate when he found himself cornered.

It was about twenty minutes after Chambrun had talked about matching evil with evil.

Chambrun and I walked down the hall to the door of Suite F, directly across the hall from the Watsons'. Chambrun rang the bell and after a moment or two the door was opened and one of the quadruplets faced us.

"Oh, Mr. Chambrun," he said. "I am Fred Winston."

"I think you know who Mr. Haskell is," Chambrun said. He was smiling his best mien-host smile. "I can't tell you how sorry I am for the problems we've created for you."

"It's something of a disaster," Winston said.

"I'm here to tell you that you're free to go now. We'll be happy to escort you down to the tournament rooms. Hopefully you may still be able to get back into your tournament."

Winston had to know that we were obeying instructions from the kidnappers, but, almost certainly, he didn't guess that Chambrun suspected him. He went back into the suite and called to his friends, and the other three came out into the hall.

It was as Chambrun had said. They were alike and yet not alike. I had seen two pictures of Victor Maginot and yet I couldn't pick him out. Their names were mentioned—Stein, and Lessigore, and MacMartin. They stared at us like owls, behind their spectacles. I thought it must be Stein; no, Lessigore. Was Mac-Martin tall enough? Surely not Winston. He was on the stout side.

"We'll escort you down," Chambrun said. "I'd like to avoid the press, if possible. We can keep them away from you."

"Is the case solved?" Winston asked.

"Solved," Chambrun said cheerfully.

"Who? Who killed the man?" the one identified as Lessigore asked.

"The police are not willing to release the story yet," Chambrun said. "I'm sorry. You'll know all about it soon enough. This way, gentlemen."

I thought I must be losing my mind. Surely I could pick him out after seeing the pictures. And yet these four were all the same. We walked down the hall to the bank of elevators. Chambrun pressed the button for

Car Number One. The door slid open almost instantly.

The elevator operator was Jerry Dodd. They knew who he was, of course. He had questioned them when we'd first been looking for Marilyn.

"We've still got our security people running the elevators to this floor," Chambrun said.

The elevators in the Beaumont are spacious. There were seven of us in the car when the door slid shut and yet we weren't crowded. The car started down, noiseless, and stopped. It had, I knew, stopped between floors. The quadruplets looked up, and around, and at each other, as people will in such a situation.

Jerry Dodd was leaning against the control panel, and he had taken a gun out of his pocket. He just held it loosely, aiming at no one. Chambrun's smile had turned to ice.

"This seems like a very good place to talk, Maginot," he said. He pointed a finger at the one called Stein. "Three nicely manicured pairs of hands, the card players, and yours, Maginot. Home job."

Maginot reached up and took of his glasses. "Thank God I can get rid of these; they've been turning me blind," he said. Somehow the outlines of the face in the photographs seemed to emerge. The haircut was wrong, but this was our man. "You're making a big mistake, Chambrun," he said. "I don't know how you arrived at this. I don't really care." His English was perfect, but there was a faint inflection that suggested his French origins. "But while I have no gun, like Dodd, I do hold the whip hand. I don't think you will risk the lives of the two ladies in order to trap me. It is all quite simple. Take us down, let us go, and an hour later you will be able to buy your ladies a drink in that elegant Trapeze Bar. You are a civilized man, Chambrun. That's the civilized way to deal with this emergency.''

"I may not be quite as civilized as you'd like to think, Victor," Chambrun said. "I knew your father thirty years ago, and he knew me. We were both involved in terror tactics in those days, he in Marseilles and I in Paris. We had a cause—freeing France from Nazi domination.''

"I have a cause," Maginot said. "Freeing the people of the world from domination by the rich and greedy.''

"But killing some of those people in the process, like a small and helpless child, and a friend whose stomach was turned by that violence. You are like all the other villains who try to control our existence, Victor. The end justifies the means. It is a concept that is slowly poisoning the entire universe.''

"Someday, in some other place, we can hold a discussion on ethics," Maginot said. "Now I suggest we continue on down, you set us free, and in an hour's time your women will be returned.''

"I don't believe you," Chambrun said.

"Why shouldn't you?" Maginot asked. "I have accomplished what I came here to do. All I want is to walk away from here, with an hour in which to get well away. I have no wish to harm your women, unless—''

"Unless they are no longer useful to you," Chambrun said. "Unless you decide they can identify their abductors and that would be a nuisance. So I don't believe you."

Maginot sounded very cool, very real to me. "I promise you that if you don't let us go, Mr. Chambrun, they will die, very unpleasantly."

"As it stands, I think that will happen to them whatever I do," Chambrun said. "So about the only satisfaction that is left to me, Victor, is to butcher you and your friends the way you butchered that child, and Downing, and Ghorra."

"Ghorra was a pig," Maginot said. "A double-dealing, lying, greedy pig."

"The child was sweet and innocent, and Downing was a loyal friend."

"But a romantic idealist," Maginot said. He glanced around the car at his friends. "So do what you have to do, Chambrun." He was clearly convinced that he held the winning cards. Chambrun would go to the very end of the road before he gave up on Ruysdale and Carol.

"I offer you a deal," Chambrun said.

"What kind of a deal?"

"Turn over the women to me, safe and unharmed, and I will let you and your friends go."

Maginot smiled. "I am expected to believe that?"

"I am expected to believe your promise of freedom for them later? Listen to me, Victor, I have no concern for anyone involved in this except Miss Ruysdale and Miss Failes. I resent the bandits of this world as much as you do, but I resent, equally, your method of dealing with them. I am not concerned with what happens to you once I have the women safe. You will terminate a few more before someone exterminates you. The more of you on both sides who die, the purer the air. I want those two women.''

"I almost believe you," Maginot said.

"Believe me. Give me the women and I will give you your chance to escape."

"I can't do very much about it, stuck in this car between floors," Maginot said.

"I will tell you exactly what you can do," Chambrun said. "You see, I know where the women are."

Maginot's face seemed to freeze.

"Our security here in the hotel is not as ineffective as you may think, Victor," Chambrun said. "There is no way Miss Ruysdale could have been moved off the second floor without being seen. She wasn't seen, so she is still on the second floor. She isn't in my offices, she isn't in the telephone rooms, she isn't in the accounting department, she isn't in Mark's apartment. The only place she can be is in the Public Relations offices at the end of the hall which have been shut for hours. Your people have the two women there."

"If that is so, why haven't you rescued them?" Maginot asked in a flat, cold voice.

"Because the moment we smash open the doors, your people will kill the women. That's the way your minds work."

"Stalemate," Maginot said.

"It need not be," Chambrun said. "We go down to the second floor in this car. You, Victor, proceed along the hallway to the P.R. offices. You talk to your people. They send the women out. We will be waiting at the other end of the hall. We will take the women directly into my office—Mark, and Dodd, and I. The elevator is yours, the way out is free and clear."

"Into the arms of the police. Your police lieutenant knows all this."

"The police are prepared to let you go once I'm convinced the women are safe."

"If I could believe that—"

"You have to believe it, Victor."

"And if I don't?"

"Jerry will shoot you dead here in the car. You attacked us," Chambrun said. "We'll have to take our chances with a rescue."

Maginot looked around at the three bridge players. It was clear the decision was his to make.

"You realize that once I reach my men in the Public Relations office I will be armed and ready to fight my way out if you are lying," he said.

Jerry Dodd looked lovingly at the gun in his hand. "Unless the women come to us safely along the hall, you'll never get the chance, buster," he said.

Maginot stared at Chambrun for a long moment.

"Let's go down to the second floor," he said.

Jerry reached behind him to the control panel and the car started its stomach-turning descent, swift and silent. At Two we stopped and the car door slid open. The hallway was deserted. The doors to the switchboard rooms and the accounting department were closed. This was not usual, but they had been forewarned.

Maginot stepped out into the hallway. The rest of us followed, Jerry first, his gun at the ready. At the far end of the hall was my office, the glass panels of the doors dark, no lights on the inside. Maginot glanced at Chambrun.

"My people may not buy this," he said.

"You had better persuade them if you want to leave this floor alive," Jerry Dodd said.

Maginot walked slowly away from us, like a man who was thinking as he moved. The hall seemed much longer than I remembered it. It took Maginot, I thought, forever to reach those closed doors. Then he rapped on one of the glass panels, and we could hear his voice but not what he said. I could feel a little trickle of sweat running down my spine as what seemed to be a lengthy argument took place. At last the door to the P.R. office opened. Maginot stood to one side.

Then they came, Ruysdale and Carol, walking straight and erect and briskly, like soldiers, looking neither right nor left.

"My office," Chambrun said sharply as they reached us.

They kept on going. I started to follow them but Chambrun's hand closed on my wrist like a vise.

"Till they are safe," he said.

I glanced at Jerry Dodd. He was half crouched, his gun cradled on his left forearm to steady it, aimed straight at Maginot. The girls turned into Chambrun's suite of offices and I heard the door close.

Chambrun raised his arm, gestured at Maginot toward the elevator, turned and headed for his office. I followed, with Jerry half backing along beside me.

In the office Carol was suddenly in my arms, crying softly. I saw Chambrun touch Ruysdale's shoulder and then walk away, facing the wall. Jerry stood by the closed door, listening.

Then came the unmistakable sound of a volley of gunshots.

Chambrun was pounding his fist against the office wall, like a man suffering some agony. He turned, and his face was the color of ashes.

"In the end they force us to tar ourselves with the same brush," he said, his voice ragged. "The end justifies the means. He forced me to lie to him." He looked around from one to the other of us. "You know he left me no choice, don't you?"

Jerry, who had stepped out into the hall, came back. He looked a little shaken himself. "It's all over," he said. "Hardy took them."

Chambrun turned and walked quickly into his private office. I disengaged myself from Carol and started to follow him.

"Let him alone, Mark," Miss Ruysdale said quietly. "He needs time to get to live with himself again."

She was right, of course. She knows him better than anyone.

the Murder of Muriel Lake

SHANNON OCORK

With her infamous flair for high drama, Muriel Lake—the
bestselling queen of the dime-store murder mystery—chose
the annual Writers of Mystery convention to announce her
impending divorce from fellow mystery author Jonathan Pells.

Hours later, Muriel Lake was dead, crushed by an avalanche
of fallen books, one outstretched hand clutching a volume
of her latest bestseller, desperate, in a death grip.

Naturally, at a convention of mystery writers, everyone
assumes murder. Rumors of a missing manuscript and a
secret lover fuel already ripe imaginations—especially that
of Cecila Burnett, a budding young novelist who discovers
she's not only good at penning mysteries, but at solving
them, as well…if she only lives long enough to tell the tale.

Don't miss these Worldwide Mysteries from award-winning authors!

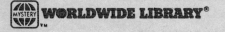

"Nothing is more satisfying than a mystery concocted by one of the pros." —*L.A. Times*

Hugh Pentecost
Winner of the Mystery Writers of America Award

TIME OF TERROR $3.50 ☐
The elegant calm of New York's plush Hotel Beaumont is shattered when a heavily-armed madman plants bombs in the building and holds two guests hostage. Manager Pierre Chambrun's only chance is to outwit the ruthless killer at his own game.

BARGAIN WITH DEATH $3.50 ☐
Pierre Chambrun, legendary manager of Hotel Beaumont has only hours to find the answers to some lethal questions when a ruthless killer turns the hotel into a deathtrap.

REMEMBER TO KILL ME $3.50 ☐
Pierre Chambrun must cope with the shooting of a close friend, a hostage situation and a gang of hoods terrorizing guests.

NIGHTMARE TIME $3.50 ☐
After the disappearance of an Air Force major involved in the Star Wars program, Chambrun must use some extraordinary measures to decide whether the disappearance is an act of treason or the hotel is harboring a killer with diplomatic immunity.

Total Amount	$ _____
Plus 75¢ Postage	.75
Payment Enclosed	$ _____

A WORM OF DOUBT

M.R.D. Meek has a "fine writing style and brilliant talent for plot."
—*Mystery News*

M.R.D. MEEK

Lennox Kemp tried never to judge on initial impression. But when the sharp-eyed Mrs. Frelis Lorimer decides Kemp is just the man to help her get rid of her husband's lovely young mistress, Kemp's immediate mistrust of the woman is well-founded. Frelis knows secrets from Lennox's past...and she's not above using blackmail to get her way.

But the hands of fate—or rather a killer—intervene. Poor Eileen is found dead in the motel jacuzzi where she'd been waiting for her lover—Frelis's husband. As the police sort out the muddle of clues, another murder occurs...and Lennox Kemp is drawn into a family mystery as perplexing as it is utterly unsettling.

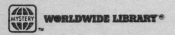